THE VILLAGE

a novel

THE CERISTEN SERIES
BOOK TWO

THE VILLAGE

a novel

VERITY A. BUCHANAN

AMBASSADOR INTERNATIONAL
GREENVILLE, SOUTH CAROLINA & BELFAST, NORTHERN IRELAND
www.ambassador-international.com

The Village

The Ceristen Series, Book Two

ISBN: 978-1-64960-023-3
eISBN: 978-1-64960-024-0
Library of Congress Control Number: 2020947857

Cover Design & Typesetting by Hannah Nichols
Ebook Conversion by Anna Riebe Raats
Edited by Daphne Self

AMBASSADOR INTERNATIONAL
Emerald House
411 University Ridge, Suite B14
Greenville, SC 29601, USA
www.ambassador-international.com

AMBASSADOR BOOKS
The Mount
2 Woodstock Link
Belfast, BT6 8DD, Northern Ireland, UK
www.ambassadormedia.co.uk

The colophon is a trademark of Ambassador, a Christian publishing company.

DEDICATION

To Peace

You knew that Arwinar needed to be cut long before I did.

THE GREY LANDS
EDEL HARTHE
FEARNISH MOUNTAINS
TO TOR HIM
FEARNLAND
HAVGEN MOUNTAINS
EDIVERNEL
THE GREAT WASTE
THAREN FALLS
HARCALAN
GALTHA RELDA
EYENA MOUNTAINS
RIVER FALGANU
MORANN
EKTSVILLE
MENEVACE
HAROTHA
SEA OF PHERITRA
ELVARRE
ERAHAR
RAESIR
CASCADE MOUNTAINS
GONTLAND
DROUHA
RIVER LANERA
EDU RIVER
RODRON
DIRION
ORDEN
REHIRNE
ELERIEN MOUNTAINS
Territory of the Northern Sunsteri
MATTADON
VELIA RIVER
RAESIR MOUNTAINS
SATHDEL ARON
Territory of the Southern Sunsteri
MESOREMN
DIRION RIVER
RUNNICOR
TERRAGERE
COASTAL SUNSTERI
BAY OF ARAHAD
ARAHAD
WALIR RIVER
ZAGHA BOWL
GLUMINTOR
STRAITS OF GLUMINTOR
ENYDHWYN
BARRO MOUNTAINS
EITHIR GULEF
HAELOR SEA
Being a map of
The KNOWN WORLD, showing the lands north of the FALLEN CONTINENT as far as EDEL HARTHE and the HAVGEN MOUNTAINS
Legea
N
W
E
S
TO HANIS

PREFACE

Dear reader,

Thank you for this moment of your time. If you picked this book up, it's probably not too much to assume that you read *The Journey* and want more of the same. As an author, I maintain the indomitable and foolhardy hope that my sequel will deliver on those expectations, but how same is "same"?

You'll find familiar characters and familiar themes in these pages. However, you'll also see an expansion of focus: more themes, more perspectives, and—most of all—more characters. While *The Journey* covered several thousand miles, this book is contained within a radius of no more than five. *The Journey* had a straightforward plot, while this one is perceptibly complex.

The Journey, you see, was the story of a family.

This is the story of a village.

—Verity A. Buchanan

CHARACTERS IN THIS BOOK

CERISTEN: NEWCOMERS

THORNE

Fred, Isabelle, Daren, Marjorie, Sandy, Cecelia, Gwenda

This family—fractured and struggling at the start of *The Journey*—has been tested by trouble, grown in their love for one another, and settled happily into the welcoming village of Ceristen.

DELANEY

Charles and Marjorie

Charles Delaney joined the Thornes toward the end of their journey to Orden and has found a happy bride in Marjorie.

KING

Braegon, Mirda, Filian

The Kings hail from far-off Fearnland. They have lived in Orden for about six months and are well-beloved among the village.

SEGELAS

Bardrick, Peony, Fiona, Marcus

Children of an Eraharian noble who deserted them and his lands, they were ousted from their status by the steward and sought refuge in Orden. A close, loving family unit, they are content to live among peasantry and do not regret what they have left behind.

Kenhelm

Mordred, Fenris, Laufeia

Young though they are, the Kenhelms have already seen both want and cruelty. They come to Orden in hope of better, but their transition is not easy.

CERISTEN: ORIGINAL INHABITANTS

Earle

Arad and Alith; Jared, Samantha, Marianne, Lia, Philip

A peaceful family. Mr. Earle is widely respected among the townsfolk and often acts as a spokesman for them.

Mogra

Syrinna; Julius and Samantha

Syrinna Mogra is widowed. Julius, her only son, is married to Samantha Earle.

Boccin

Lucas and Lissa; Gallert, Molly, Linda

Figures of small importance in the story. Lissa is Alith Earle's sister.

Denholm

Kenneth, Jerithan

The Denholms were orphaned when Kenneth was fourteen and Jerithan a babe in arms. Since then, Kenneth has struggled to protectively raise his wayward younger brother. He is courting Marianne Earle with serious intentions.

STAFFORD

Edrach and Kirade; Ferenia, Legola, Maira, Vitty, Lowell

Figures of small importance in the story. The youngest entire family in Ceristen. Their oldest daughter is married to a carpenter in Orden City.

GREY

Gorun and Galina; Ledelia, Therelane, Irene, Lewis, Adolphus, Cormad

The Greys are a cursed family. Rich and secluded, they remain in their house, avoiding contact with the villagers. But those whom the curse does not affect begin to chafe at the walls of separation.

OTHER CHARACTERS

COLIM

The foreman who oversees the repair work on the old castle.

UNNAMED WOMAN

Tall and strange, she inhabits the abandoned Grey dwelling unknown to any of the villagers.

CAPTAIN FINLEY RHODES

Comes to check on the progress of the castle repairs every few weeks.

CHAPTER ONE

LILTING PIPE MUSIC WHISTLED BRIGHT and clear, diving and swooping in a lively ripple of sound. Light and laughter swung past, young men with maidens on their arms, as the tense gaiety of the dance gathered, spun, and circled back again.

She sat apart from it, her slender fingers knitting together in her lap. *Had Marcus not said he would come?*

Her younger brother's teasing face surfaced to her memory, the infectious smile tilting up the corners of his lips. "Come, sister, why not?"

"You ought to, Fiona." Peony's fair features settled into lines of affected maturity. "What with making this cottage clean and livable, I am far too busy to attend myself; but 'twould be most proper for you to mingle with young people your age, and I can easily spare your help for the evening."

"Yes, Peony." Her sister was right. "But I—"

"How foolish of me!" Marcus smacked a hand dramatically against his forehead. "If Peony doesn't come, you will have no one to keep you company. But Fiona, that's easily mended: I'll come myself. They can't mean to start till the castle work is finished, unless for some outlandish reason the foreman lets them all off early. So I shall meet you there, if not directly, at least soon after you arrive. Perhaps I can convince Bardrick to come as well!"

She gave his expectant face an answering smile. "All right, then."

But Marcus had not come.

Believing that he would arrive soon, wanting to wait unnoticed for his arrival, she had slipped into the room and seated herself in a dim corner by the wall where no one seemed to go. Now, longing for company and yet afraid to go out and find it, she remained on her chair and watched the merry, vigorous throng—trapped just outside that thrumming web of fellowship.

She ought to go home. But if she moved now, someone would surely see her. Oh, she wanted to be seen, wanted to talk, to be full of Peony's social grace and poise.

I do not know what I want, she admitted to herself. Blinking away the unshed tears, she lowered her eyes from the dancing circle.

~

He shut his eyes to absorb the music in its full purity of sound. It coursed through his senses, building and rushing like a spring-high river. Softly he hummed with it, his ear picking out the guiding harmony in the rapid flurry of notes.

Then all at once it ended, and Fred looked up as the twirling group fell apart in laughter and shouting and formed a triumphant circle around the glowing bride and groom.

"Long life to Marjorie Delaney!" cried someone, and Fred, with a smile breaking over his face, came forward to accept the cup that Braegon King was holding out to him. He gave it to Marjorie, who drank a brief draught and set it in his hands to do likewise. Then Charles held out his hands in turn, and they repeated the demonstration.

Several girls leaped forward to scatter dried flowers and fir needles over Marjorie's head as she shrank back laughing against Charles. Then they seized the bride's wrists to lead her into yet another dance. She waved her hand in a brief farewell to Fred, and he watched her go with a smile on his lips and his heart full of her gladness.

"What better way to welcome you into the village than with marriage festivities for the whole village to attend?" Braegon had exclaimed when Fred mentioned to him his sister's betrothal.

"I do not feel unwelcomed," Fred answered amusedly.

Braegon sputtered and made a dismissive gesture. "That is well, my friend, but how often does the opportunity arise in the middle of winter for celebration? The village would be outraged if we did not!"

"And considering it is the middle of winter, have you a solution for where to gather all the town together?" Fred inquired.

"Of course," rejoined Braegon instantly; "the common threshing floor. 'Tis used for any such occasion."

Fred smiled in acquiescence. "Then it will make me glad to rejoice with you and the others on that day, Braegon."

Now his gaze roamed over the room, seeking out faces that he recognized. There was Cecelia, her usual reserve fallen away from her face in the dance; Isabella, chattering to Braegon's sister; and Sandy, beside a girl whose hair rivaled scarlet berries in its shade. Fred remembered her as one of the Earle daughters, though he could not recall her name. Her red hair was pulled back into a smooth coil behind her head, and her clear, pale cheeks flushed slightly as she pointed to someone beyond Fred's line of sight.

Where was Gwenda, though? She had not wanted to leave his side on their arrival, but now he realized he had not seen her since the ceremony itself ended and the dancing began. But he found Gwenda, too, in a corner apart from the dancers, on her knees across from a young boy. She leaned forward, black locks falling over her shoulders and her pointed face serious but quite at ease. Satisfied, Fred looked away.

Then he saw her, a figure all but concealed in the shadows of the far corner. And at once he wondered who she was, bewildered at her quietude and her separation.

"Braegon? Braegon." He caught the other's arm as he passed. "That woman in the corner, who is she and why is she alone?"

Braegon looked. "I do not know," he answered in surprise. "Nay, wait. I think she may be of the Segelas family. They came to Ceristen yesterday, do you not remember? Bardrick."

"Aye, I do remember Bardrick."

"He had two sisters and a brother. I would guess she is one. She is certainly no one I recognize. And it looks that the poor lass has come all alone, as you say!"

"No one should be lonely on this night," said Fred firmly, and moving away from Braegon he strode across the room.

~

Fiona heard the footsteps coming her way and raised her head. It was a man, a young man, but he looked older the closer he came. Then she realized it was the gravity in his brown eyes that made him old; that, and the careful, quiet bearing that one more often saw in the walk of old men than young. Puzzled by his approach, the shyness surging, she almost looked away; but she was a lady of Erahar, she could hold her head.

"You sit alone, my lady." He spoke as courteously as if she had been a queen, his voice low and gentle.

She nodded. "I expected my brother, but he did not come. And I—it is not easy for me to enter the company of those I do not know."

"You are the sister of Bardrick, Bardrick Segelas?"

"Aye. I am Fiona, his youngest sister."

"I am Frederick Thorne, but lately arrived in Ceristen myself. That is my sister who has just been wedded," he added with a hint of brotherly pride. Looking around a moment, he drew up another of the roughly hewn wooden chairs that were scattered nearby and seated himself. "I met Bardrick yesterday; you are of gentry?"

"A noble's house of Erahar we once were. When my other brother was young, our father and mother disappeared. The steward Froeda took control and we were treated as servants. A year ago, my brother said 'Enough', and wanted to take back what was ours, but word reached Froeda's ears and he would have retaliated with worse than servitude. So we left."

"Then yours has been a longer journey than mine," he said, regarding her seriously. "I departed Harotha with my own family four months since and reached Orden in the last days of December."

"It was a slow journey," she assented, "but an easy one all the same."

His face warmed in an answering smile. "That is well; long and easy may be preferable above short and troublesome!"

"Was yours so difficult then?" she asked, her brows lifting in question.

"Difficult? My lady Fiona, those who have heard it call it a miracle we are here at all!"

Suddenly she found that he was laughing gently, and she was laughing with him. A warmth flew up into her cheeks, but a greater happiness flooded her heart. The dreadful loneliness had fled, and she was content.

"Come," Frederick Thorne said, standing. "You cannot stay here on such a joyous night as this." He held out his hand to lift her up and gestured out into the circle of light. "There are few enough families here; it will not be a trial to introduce you to them. There is Earle, Stafford, Boccin, Denholm, and King, and finally a young man, Julius Mogra, who is married to Mr. Earle's daughter."

"Julius *Ogre*!" Fiona observed in surprise, before she thought.

Frederick Thorne looked at her, silent, not understanding.

"I," she stammered, ashamed. "Never mind." How could she explain and not seem patronizing, as though she were above his like?

"No," he interposed quickly, gently. "Tell me . . . please." She saw a soft fire, a subdued and yet passionate eagerness, awakening in his eyes.

And wondering, she answered. "'Mogra' is of the language that the old Ordenians spoke, Frederick Thorne. It means monster or ogre. The great trolls of the mountains are still called Mogra."

"Ah," he breathed, and said no more for a moment. Then he looked down at her. "Call me Fred. Frederick I do like, but Fred I am used to."

"As you wish—Fred."

"There, now we are coming along well." His eyes smiled teasingly, though his face was still sober. After a moment she gave him a small, answering smile.

"Come, Fiona Segelas," he said, taking her hand again. "Let me show the people of Ceristen to you."

~

Not far from the threshing floor, three tired figures came to a halt under the starlight.

"We are lost." It was the girl who spoke in weary exasperation. "I told you we should not have walked past sundown."

"I thought we were near to Orden City," returned the tallest sharply. "We should have come to it, I am certain, if we followed the road."

"I think it is plain, Mordred, that we are not on the road anymore. If we had only halted when I suggested, instead of pressing on because we were 'so close'—"

"Let us keep walking a little further."

"Mordred, enough! You have said that for the past three hours! We are not walking any further. Next thing you know we will walk into a bear den."

"Hardly likely."

"Mordred, I do not know what you are made of, but Fenris can scarcely go any further, and neither can I."

"Wait, Laufeia."

"No!"

"No, wait! Do you see that?"

"What?"

A short while later they stood in front of the dark building lit from within, listening to the cheerful sounds emanating from its walls.

"That is something, at any rate." Mordred moved forward to the doorway and turned the handle slowly, looking in, the others close behind him. And there they stood, wondering what to do next.

~

It was Braegon who saw the wary, uncertain forms waiting just without. He hurried towards them with quick stride, curiosity furrowing his brow. "Aye? Are you from down the mountain?"

'Twas a foolish question, he scolded himself. They would not understand his meaning—Orden City—and they were certainly not from anywhere on the mountain.

"I told you we were walking uphill!" The shortest of the three, a girl with a long braid of fine, pale hair, cast a sharp look at her much taller companion.

He ignored her. "Sir, are we near Orden City?"

Braegon laughed. "Near, if you count a four hours' walk near. You cannot go anywhere tonight. Come within and join us in the wedding celebration; and if you must have a place to room tonight, I can surely take you myself."

He led them in firmly. "You have been traveling far?"

Under the shadow of the night they had all looked alike: tired, thin, pale with cold. Now, however, he could see the strong differences between them, and paradoxically a heightened similarity, strengthening his first guess that they were siblings. The two young men were dark-haired, their eyes wide-set and grey in clear-cut faces, yet aside from that their resemblance was slight. The older, shedding his hesitant air at the door, walked with an easy, confident grace, his head thrown back a little and his eyes alert and challenging. His brother, about Braegon's own height, lacked any such assurance in his manner; his slender features were almost anxious, his eyes shy.

As for the girl, her hair, which he had thought flaxen in the dimness, gleamed faintly reddish in the light, a bright contrast to her brother's dark heads. Her features were a striking mirror to the taller man's, but her chin bore an even more adamant set than his.

"I am Mordred Kenhelm," the tall young man said with a slight nod. "These are my brother and sister, Fenris and Laufeia. We have come far, yes; from Rehirne, to the south."

"I know very little of the south," admitted Braegon with a wry grin. "I came from Fearnland in the north, and that is where my learning centered."

"Then Rehirne will be very south to you," said Mordred with an unexpected out-flashing of quick humor.

Braegon laughed. "Indeed!"

"Is there good work for finding in Orden City?" questioned the girl; her stern tone suggested that she was used to reminding her brother of the matter at hand.

"I am rarely down in Orden City," answered Braegon. "But I can tell you that you are welcome to stay here. 'Tis as fair work as you will find anywhere else, unless you are a skilled artisan. The old cottages are good for use, at least with a little repair that the village will be glad to aid you in."

"And the work? We cannot farm in the winter, unless all this snow is an illusion," Mordred remarked.

"That it is not," Braegon assured him with a snort. "Nay, I meant the rebuilding of the old castle, which is to be soon inhabited again by a baron."

"It seems good," said Mordred thoughtfully, looking around. "We shall consider, certainly."

~

"They are so friendly, so welcoming." The smile echoed in Fiona's voice as she shook her head in wonder.

Fred smiled too. *How could they not be?*

He had approached the dim corner, seen a slender, shadowy figure and a coronet of bright hair wound around her head. Then she raised her eyes and he was struck by the poise in that one movement, the straightness of her shoulders and the graceful, proud lift of her head. He had thought of Cecelia then. Yet the girl's bearing was that of one to whom nobility has been inbred from birth, as indeed it had.

So his appreciation for loveliness had been quickened instantly. But loveliness was one thing, knowledge another, and in their discourse, he had quickly perceived the vast sea of learning behind her simple words. He could not help a sense of pride as he led her among the villagers, for he felt like one who has discovered a treasure, a pearl alighted on the dark sands of the sea.

"There is Braegon," he said aloud, noticing the familiar slim dark figure nearby.

"Fred!" exclaimed Braegon. "I have been wondering where you were."

"And I you," Fred answered, smiling. "And these?" he asked, seeing the three strangers standing behind Braegon.

"They are travelers whom I am endeavoring to sway to my point of view," said Braegon with a laugh, "that Ceristen is the place they ought to settle."

"You say so as though you were having difficulty," said the tall young man, his grey eyes teasing under an unruly lock of black hair; "when the truth is, you have all but persuaded us. I asked only the night to think it over, did I not?"

Braegon conceded with a shrug. "The Kenhelm family," he introduced them, "Mordred, Laufeia, and—? I have forgotten."

"And Fenris," said Mordred. His tone was suddenly very soft.

Fred looked at the lad in question. He could not have been more than a few years below than his brother, maybe sixteen or seventeen, yet he seemed much the younger; and more than that, a fear lay latent somewhere in him, manifesting just barely in his face. But in his eyes, as he looked at Mordred, there was undiminished love and trust.

~

"Farewell, my lady Fiona." The firm touch of Fred Thorne's hand was warm on her shoulder as she walked out the door into the night. The warm light streaming past her cast the gleam of gold on the snow, growing weaker and weaker until it straggled away into grey shadow. Then she was walking in the night, but the stars were out and she knew the way.

The night was calm—a calm, white, hard winter's night— the stars bright and the sky black and the air very still, nothing breathing save the trees, which creaked stiffly with the cold. She was halfway home when something stirred on the edge of the path.

Fiona's heart flew up to choke her breath, the thought of wolves seizing her mind. But a human figure stepped out onto the path, a woman, clad in a long cloak. She waited, poised on the edge, looking furtively to the right and the left, and with one long stride was halfway across the path.

Then she checked sharply and turned to stare at Fiona, and what she did next frightened Fiona more than anything else—she whirled with a bound into the trees. The dark cloak flowed about her and whipped out of sight.

Why should she flee like that? What is she doing? Why did she run? Fiona pulled her shawl close and hurried along the dark path, breaking into a run. She did not slow until she reached the house.

CHAPTER TWO

BARDRICK LOOKED UP AS FIONA flung the door open and came in. Her blue eyes were wide and dark, her heavy braid fallen from its crown around her head.

"Fiona, are you all right?"

She nodded, catching her breath by the door. "Aye. It was nothing; I—I was startled on the road is all."

"Did you enjoy yourself? When we returned you were gone, and I thought to go after you, but we were so busy caring for Marcus."

"Marcus!" she cried. "What happened to Marcus?"

Bardrick held up his hand. "No need to fear, Fiona. He slipped on the ice in the courtyard and sprained his ankle; it will mend soon enough. He is sleeping now."

"Is that Fiona?" called a voice in the darkness of the room opposite.

Fiona with a smile let slide her shawl and hurried towards it; Bardrick followed, foresightedly taking a candle with him.

"Marcus, how does it feel?" Fiona queried, kneeling by the cot and prodding the bandage around her younger brother's leg.

Marcus grinned. "All the better for your ministrations, sister. Really, Fiona, you'd think I was at death's door. As a matter of fact, it didn't hurt much at all after Peony tied it up tight and I could get my weight off it properly. And I hope you had a lovely time?"

Fiona's shoulders quivered. "A lovely time!" she burst out, casting Marcus a look of disbelief. "After you promised to meet me to keep me from being lonely, the only reason I came, Marcus, you can ask me if I—"

She broke off as Bardrick laid a hand on her shoulder. In a moment she resumed gravely. "I'm sorry, Marcus. I didn't mean to be so upset. As a matter of fact, it was all right, and I did have a lovely time, though I hadn't expected to. I was lonely at first, so lonely, but the brother of the bride, Frederick Thorne, saw me and spoke to me awhile, and made me quite at ease. He was very kind." Her eyes softened with the memory, and a happy smile parted her lips.

One of Marcus' eyebrows quirked slowly up. In the silence, Fiona caught his expression, and gave him a puzzled look.

"You . . . liked this Frederick fellow?" Marcus said.

Bardrick sighed. "Marcus—"

"No, wait," said Marcus, waving his hand imperiously. "This is most interesting. Did you kiss him, Fiona?"

Fiona stood indignantly. "Marcus Segelas! I am not the daughter of a knave and a vagabond—nor yet are you the son of one, though one would think otherwise from your words. He but took pity on my friendless state, and certainly made no inappropriate advances to me! Nor am I attracted towards him, except insofar as he is gentlemanly and pleasant company."

"So you are attracted to him!"

"Marcus, enough," said Bardrick as Fiona whirled and fled the room. He looked in disapproval at his younger brother.

Marcus shrugged helplessly. "It is just teasing."

"She does not handle your teasing well, and still less when she is tired." Bardrick turned with a sigh. "Perhaps you will find a girl yourself someday. 'Twould serve you right." He left.

~

"Now are we never going to live with Marjorie again?" asked Gwenda with a sad appeal in her dark eyes as they breakfasted.

"Someday, maybe. It is not likely to happen soon," answered Fred sympathetically. "We may still see her often, especially when spring comes."

"But why?" Gwenda protested.

"She will want to live with her husband now, little sister."

"Then cannot Charles live here?" Gwenda asked reasonably.

"While he is assistant to the blacksmith, it is more practical for him to live in the smith's house," explained Fred.

Gwenda sighed. "I suppose when you marry, you will leave too?"

Daren laughed. "We men, if we marry, Gwenda, will take our wives home with us."

"They will not make up for Marjorie," said Gwenda regretfully.

"I'll miss Marjorie too," said Sandy, rising. "Now I've got no one to mend all my ripped things for me, and I shall have to be useful." She took out a heavy wool skirt and set to darning with a ferocious energy.

~

The wooden bowl was worn with many vigorous scrubbings, but not a crack marred its sturdy curves. Laufeia traced her fingers over it, set it down, and rose with her brother as their young host turned toward the door.

"Braegon," Mordred called after him. "Where can we acquire this castle work?"

Braegon turned, his smile flashing out. "Then you have decided?"

"There is no reason not to stay, as long as you are sure you can find us a house."

"They are quite old, all of them," Braegon acknowledged, "and some are nothing more than a pile of rubble. But with a bit of searching we should be able to find one that will do you. The village will be glad to help you patch it up as much as needed."

"Thank you," said Laufeia, nudging Mordred.

He twitched away in annoyance. "Aye, thank you, sir."

"I am not a sir," said Braegon laughingly, throwing up a hand. "You must be my senior by a year or more."

Her brother's stiff face relaxed at the easy humor, a thin brow flickering up in response. "Scarcely, I think. I am eighteen."

"There you are. I will not reach that mark until July. At any rate," he continued, "concerning work, you need only come with me to the castle. We will see how the foreman takes yet another addition to his crew."

A girl of sixteen came out of the bedroom, slim and dark like Braegon, twisting her curls into a braid. "You are leaving now, Braegon?"

"Aye, Mirda. I'll take us by the Earles, to let them know of your decision," he added to Mordred. "Mr. Earle will know of a suitable house, and then the womenfolk can help get it cleaned for you by the time we come home tonight."

"Fenris," Mordred called over his shoulder. "Come, we're to leave now."

The door shut behind the three young men, and Laufeia passed a hand over her head with a sigh, feeling suddenly quite tired, though she had slept past sunrise this morning.

Not to mention dirty.

"Laufeia?"

Laufeia looked up and met Mirda's gaze. The girl's smile was much like her brother's, so open and joyful. They had seen one another several times last night, and she had warmed to the other girl's sunny presence at once. But thinking back to last night was like thinking of last year, it was all so fuzzy now. "Aye?"

Mirda produced a comb and handed it to her. "I thought you might like to use this," she said with a cheerful, woman-to-woman attitude. "And while you're doing that, I'll melt some snow over the fire for you to wash up a bit with." And the smile sprang out again.

Laufeia hesitated a moment and returned the smile. "Thank you," she said, tugging the string from the end of her braid. When was the last time she had undone it?

Slowly she unraveled the reddish strands with her fingers and began to work the comb through them. When Mirda returned with a faintly steaming bowl of water, she was shaking it back over her shoulders in readiness to braid again.

"Oh, what beautiful long hair you have!" Mirda, in feminine appreciation, moved over to stroke it as Laufeia eagerly plunged her hands in the water. "Has it ever been cut?"

"I don't know," answered Laufeia, laughing a little. She picked up the rag that Mirda had set nearby and scrubbed fiercely at her neck. "Not since I can remember. Since it reaches near my feet now, I usually keep it braided."

Mirda laughed understandingly. "Aye. Do you mind if I braid it?"

"Of course not!" said Laufeia. "Just do it tightly. I often leave it in for days at a time."

"It must have been a hard journey, yours?" asked Mirda.

Laufeia did not answer directly, enjoying the sensation of Mirda's sure fingers slipping smoothly through her hair and pulling taut. "Hard. We—"

She paused.

“We came from Rehirne.”

Mirda’s hands halted and rested warm for a moment against Laufeia’s back. “Oh?” she said sympathetically.

Laufeia floundered a moment, suddenly unsure whether she wanted to go on, even to Mirda’s kind ears. “We . . . we found it hard to earn our way. After crossing into Dirion, it grew easier—yet even then—”

“You must be glad to be in Orden at last,” said Mirda.

“It seems like a dream,” said Laufeia.

Silence rested between them for a little.

“There, it is done,” said Mirda, letting the finished braid fall. “Shall we walk to the Earles now? We can find your new house and help them clean it up.”

“Yes,” said Laufeia, turning. “I would certainly want to be a part of that.”

~

“Will you come in?” Braegon asked as he paused outside the Earle’s door.

Mordred thought a moment and shook his head. “We’ll wait.” He paced slowly across the frozen path. Braegon disappeared within.

“Why are you not happy, Mordred?” Fenris’ quiet eyes studied him.

Mordred looked up with surprise. “Fenris?”

“You don’t pace unless something is bothering you,” said Fenris simply.

Mordred smiled in a moment of delighted pride at his brother’s discernment. Then he faded into pensiveness. “Nothing, really. It feels too easy, I suppose. Everything falls into place so well. Nothing is this easy.”

"Maybe for some people it is," said Fenris, a slight plea in his soft voice.

Mordred looked at him. "I don't want it to be hard. Not for you, Fenris. It won't be, I promise."

Braegon returned, beckoning them to follow, and they reached the castle by midmorning. The sun was bright but cold, and the biting wind of January cut past them, wailing in the broken stones of the keep as they entered.

"The foreman," said Braegon, pointing as the man with bristling brown beard and judicial eye approached them.

"What is it?" demanded the man, folding his arms forbiddingly. "You're late, Braegon King."

"I am sorry, sir." Braegon bowed his head respectfully. "These are Mordred and Fenris Kenhelm, and they are here to stay."

"More, eh? Don't know where you're picking all these up. Prisons? Slums?"

"Sir." Mordred's voice was suddenly cold as the penetrating wind. "I do not see the call for such insulting remarks."

"Get used to it." The foreman shrugged. "Start carting off that rubble."

Mordred's chin jerked up, his lips hardening into a thin line. "I did not expect to come here and be disparaged and ordered like a slave," he said in a tone so effusively polite that it bordered on insolence. "It might be considered courteous to apologize—"

"Mordred," said Braegon gently. "He did not mean it."

"I won't have that kind of talk from you, young riffraff," growled the foreman. "Shut it and start work."

"Oh—riffraff, am I?" Mordred's chin tilted higher. "I see."

"Boy," said the foreman dangerously, "you and that skinny stripling behind you can move along and get to work."

Mordred went rigid.

"You will not speak so of my brother," he said in a soft, angry voice.

"Oh? Well, you know what, you haughty little brat? I've had it. I won't have your kind over here. You can go look somewhere else for a job." The foreman turned flatly away.

"Now wait just a moment, sir." Mordred strode after him and caught him by the shoulder.

"Mordred!" Fenris cried out.

Mordred turned briefly. "Fenris, go ahead and leave while I handle this."

"Mordred, please—"

"Fenris, it will be fine. Just go away for now and come back in a little while." Mordred spoke with a gentle but masterful air.

Fenris' lips moved as though he might speak again, but at last he turned and walked out of the courtyard.

~

"You're hired." The growl rang off the cracked west wall, echoing back into the enclosure so that heads turned and eyes lifted. "Now get out of here. I don't want to see your face again before tomorrow."

Braegon glanced at Mordred, who wheeled with that small, arrogant lift of the head and strode toward the gate. Yet his haughty attitude vanished almost at once, and he glanced about distractedly, halting by Braegon. "Fenris," he murmured, "where is Fenris? Has he not returned?"

"Not that I have seen," Braegon answered. He had to crane his neck back to look Mordred in the eye.

A troubled look flickered through Mordred's withdrawn gaze, quenched just as swiftly. "I will wait for him by the gate."

Braegon nodded and returned to his chiseling.

~

Laufeia spun around in the little room, feeling the space all around, smelling the damp pine logs that Mr. Earle had dumped in the fireplace, seeing the dark beams overhead, and the rough table and chairs that he and Jared had left behind them.

A house. It was hers.

"I know just how you feel," said Mirda happily, watching her drink in the glorious sight. "Braegon said, 'It's not much, Mirda'; but I told him, 'What do you mean, not much? It's a new house. I've never had my own house before!'"

"Yes," said Laufeia, stroking the handle freshly fitted to the door, scuffing the smooth-swept dirt floor under her feet. "That's exactly how I feel about it."

Mirda giggled. "Do you know, Laufeia, every time you twirl, I want to tug that braid of yours? It swings so alluringly!"

A giggle of her own pushed up inside Laufeia and almost made its way out. It startled her; she could not remember the last time she had wanted to laugh so freely.

The door creaked open and Laufeia jumped back from it. Mordred's tall frame was in the doorway. Even in the evening light, she could see how white his face was.

"Laufeia," he said.

"Mordred?" She uttered the question, knowing there could only be one thing that would make him look like that.

"Fenris is missing."

"Fenris missing? But—but how—" Lightheadedness tumbled about her for a moment before sensibility regained control. "Mordred, it may not be as bad as—"

"Don't talk to me like that!" he cried. His grey eyes sparked with anger. "Don't tell me what is bad and what—"

"We've searched the mountainside for hours," said Braegon quietly, his voice cutting under Mordred's tirade as he approached with a lantern. "I'm fearing he may have gone into the Wilds, Mirda."

"The Wilds?" Laufeia faltered, looking from Braegon's keen dark eyes to Mirda's frightened blue ones.

"The northeast slope of the mountain." All the ordinary cheer was gone from Braegon's attitude, his face was unsmiling and grim as a soldier's, yet he seemed oddly in the right place: calm, in command, attuned to the moment. "That is the place where the dark beasts that ravaged Thiranu in the old days came from. There's wild animals that fester there now, and other, worse things."

"Fenris is—" But Laufeia could not finish her sentence.

"We fear so," said Braegon. "But we may find him somewhere else. Even if he has wandered into the Wilds, that is not a death sentence. Fear not, Laufeia. We'll find him yet."

You must. Laufeia looked at her brother's pale, set face, the agony behind his eyes. *For his sake, you must . . .*

~

Fred saw the slatted gleam of the lantern as it swung in his brother's hand, and then the weary stoop of his shoulders. "No one has found him, Daren?"

Daren shook his head. "Braegon said to go northeast, towards the Wilds, you know."

"The Wilds?" Fred echoed. With a sinking heart he turned and led the way through the heavy snow. Their footsteps rustled and crunched in the night.

Suddenly Daren exclaimed softly, and Fred dropped to one knee, peering at the marks they both had seen. Footprints, one solitary string, winding over the whiteness. Fred took the lantern and raised it to reveal the aimless trail until it disappeared into a dark overhang of firs.

"I will take the light and go after them," he said, rising swiftly. "Hurry back and tell the others what we have found, Daren."

"Aye, Fred." Their eyes met. "My brother, be careful."

Fred nodded and broke the gaze, heading into the trees.

The green-black pine branches whipped against his face; the yellow lantern-light sent split beams searching wildly through the forest, creating elusive, deformed shadows. At last he broke their cover and came out on the edge of a steep bluff; and he hesitated, but there the footprints led.

Painstakingly he edged his way down the ridge, doubtless passable in daylight, but now it was a nightmare. All at once his footing gave out under him and he toppled, the lantern sailing from his hand. Skidding, rolling, tumbling, he struck a hard surface and felt it split under him with a loud crack.

His body knew instinctively before his mind could comprehend, and with a desperate lunge he launched himself forward into the snow. Struggling to catch his breath, he stumbled up to his feet again. He stared at the splintered gap in the frozen surface of the creek.

He looked this way and that, searching for the lantern, but it was useless. All he could do was climb up the other side of the ravine and hope there was enough light to go by.

The rising moon lent a dead glow to the white, stick-like birches as he gained the top. They were scattered sparsely all over the rises around, claWing up into the hazy, silvered sky. And the tracks that he had been following all this time led under the branches of the nearest cluster.

He blinked a moment as he stepped among them, the shadows and moon-light casting strange illusions on his eyes before things righted themselves and he saw it. Disarray of snapped limbs and scraped bark, trampled snow all around his feet.

Uncertain what to think, and afraid, he bent to look closer. It was hard to read anything at all, especially by the poor light, but he could see that the whole thicket was disturbed; and there was a second set of tracks, he did not know what of, but they were massive. Maybe a bear, or a panther. A panther was more likely in the dead of winter, but by the degree of crushing that the trees had suffered, it could well have been an awakened bear.

Fred hurried forward, hope plummeting like a rock through his stomach and leaving a sense of sickness in its wake. He looked for a carcass, for bones, for blood—he felt in the cold, soft snow with his hands. Yet there was nothing.

Everywhere, nothing.

Hesitantly, the hope rekindled. There must be some trace if the animal had made his kill, must there not?

But if there had been no kill, where was Fenris?

He crossed to the opposite side of the grove, seeking another set of tracks leading out of the trees. And then he stepped onto air and, for the second time that night, found himself sliding down a slope.

A cascade of powdery snow sifted around him as he came to a stop. Behind him the embankment loomed, dark and sheer, the top jutting in an overhang.

Fred rose, a thought flashing into his mind, wondering if this were the answer: if the bear had struck, only to knock his prey down the hidden bank. And maybe, just maybe, such a sudden snag had seemed too much, and he had turned away and not persisted in his hunt—

And there, just a little to his left, a dark form lay half-hidden in the snow.

Fred's breath flew out in a gasp of relief. "Fenris!"

He knelt and laid a hand on his neck. The boy did not stir, but his pulse was beating. Maybe just stunned in the fall. Fred hoped desperately that was all before he rolled him gently over and stared in horror.

Gashing Fenris' forehead, eye to hairline, ran a single wound. Blood still oozed from it, covering his face and clothes, though the cold had slowed what might have been a dangerous bleeding otherwise. Aside from the dark stains, his face was colorless and icy to the touch, and Fred, feeling a prickle of fear, sought his pulse again. Nay, he was alive. But he could not stay here much longer and remain so.

Fred stripped off his coat and wrapped it around Fenris' unconscious form. Then he turned and climbed up the steep bank, running back under the serene moonlight and the thin limbs of the birches. He slid down into the steep ravine and hesitated at the bottom, staring at the grey creek and the black hole in the middle. Carefully he put a foot on the ice; it hissed and shifted under him. He drew back, crouched, and leaped.

~

Daren returned to their agreed meeting-place, Braegon's house, and found him pacing with a quick, clipped stride in front of the fire.

"Braegon," he said. "We found traces of him, at least it seems so. Fred is following them now."

Braegon whirled, relief dawning in his eyes. He moved over to a small figure sitting against the wall and shook him lightly. "Filian."

Braegon's younger brother of twelve stirred and stood up drowsily, swallowing back a yawn. He looked from Braegon to Daren in perplexity.

"They've found signs of Fenris. Go out and sound the signal to the others." He handed him the horn, and Filian darted out even as a step sounded in the adjoining room and Mordred Kenhelm appeared in the doorway.

"Fenris?" he said.

"We saw his footprints," answered Daren. "At least, I do not know whose they could be other than his."

"I told you we should have news of him eventually," said Braegon, laying a steady hand on Mordred's arm.

"News is nothing," said Mordred harshly. "He may still be—" Breaking off short, he wheeled and walked back into the other room.

The other searchers began to return, waiting for Fred's arrival and further word of Fenris. Mr. Earle and his son Jared, Edrach Stafford, Lucas Boccin and his son, young Kenneth Denholm, and even Bardrick Segelas were there. Several talked in low tones of little things.

At last Braegon exclaimed, "We cannot wait longer! Something has happened to him, or he has found Fenris and is trying to bring him back on his own. Either way, he will need help—"

His words died away as the door banged open.

"Fred!" Daren cried aloud in horror.

Fred stumbled on the threshold, his clothing clinging to him and dripping icy water. Braegon sprang forward, seizing his arm and leading him to the fire. "Stay there. Filian—Filian! Get Mirda, and fetch blankets and some spare clothes of mine!"

"Fenris," gasped Fred.

"Fred, what happened?"

"Fell in—creek. But Fenris—follow my tracks—hurt."

"All right. We'll go after him; Mirda will take care of you. There you are, Filian."

"You—need—rope," Fred stammered, trying to force the words out between the shivering that was beginning to wrack his body. "Ben—eath—overha—"

"I understand," said Braegon swiftly, cutting him off. "We'll see to it, Fred; fret not. Come, Mr. Earle, Jared, Edrach; we should not need more than four or five altogether."

Mirda came running out of the room where she had been sitting with Laufeia. Braegon caught her eye, nodding to Fred, and hurried out the door with the men.

~

The fire's faint crackling was loud in the painful stillness that had settled over the room. After Braegon, Edrach, and the Earles had left, the other men drifted away back to their own homes. Mirda and Daren helped Fred to the bedroom. Mordred and Laufeia came out to wait alone by the door.

A soft creak made them both jerk up, but it was only Filian coming out of the bedroom. He surveyed them with alert dark eyes like his older brother's, and after a pause sat down beside the hissing fire, his legs crossed under him and those thoughtful eyes gazing into the red and golden depths.

Mordred looked at him and suddenly jerked away, as though something about him hurt to see.

The door opened with a noise that seemed like a snap of thunder in the silence, and Mordred took a swift pace forward as Braegon and Mr. Earle came in. They were bearing a motionless form between them; they laid him down next to the fire, and Braegon hurried into the next room. Mr. Earle set to chafing Fenris' hands.

When Mordred saw his brother's blood-streaked brow, his face turned as white as Fenris' own. He stood stone-stiff for an instant and then crossed the room in a few long strides, kneeling and lifting one of the cold hands in his. "Fenris," he whispered.

Braegon arrived with a basin of water and a linen rag, which he dipped in the water, and began to wipe the gaping cut.

"Get a needle and thread," Mr. Earle said, looking over at Braegon's work. "There's a second one, too, near his ear, but not as bad; just grazed him. Looks like something tried to claw his face. You have them, Mirda? Good. Even if they're mostly closed, it will be safer to have such cuts sewn up."

Mirda approached and held needle and thread hesitantly out to her brother, but Braegon stepped aside, shaking his head. "You'll have to, Mirda; I've never handled that."

Mirda's eyes widened. Slowly she sat and threaded the needle. Even when she put it through his skin, Fenris never flinched or stirred. His shallow breaths could barely be heard.

As Mirda finished Braegon stepped back, dashing sweat from his brow. "What of Fred, Mirda?"

Mirda carefully tucked the needle into her bodice and pressed unsteady hands together. "He is still shivering," she answered, "but it's lessened."

"Still conscious?"

"Aye."

"That is good," said Braegon with a weary sigh. He dropped down in a chair by the table, leaning his head in his hand.

Mr. Earle rose from Fenris' side. "He was not frostbitten. Keep rubbing him all over, and he will soon enough be warm again. I must be going to my own home now. Be sure to tell me how he is tomorrow, Braegon."

Braegon nodded, the movement scarcely visible. He dropped his head down onto the table, pillowing it on his arms, and when Mirda came over to him she found him sound asleep.

~

"Bardrick!" Peony cried as he shut the door behind himself. She rushed forward and seized his cold hands. "Praise to the Ruler! Where on the face of Legea have you been?"

Bardrick stamped the snow tiredly from his boots and looked from Peony to Fiona.

"Bardrick?" came Marcus' anxious query from the bedroom. "I've been trying to keep the girls calm here, but it's rather hard when one is alarmed oneself . . . "

"I'm sorry I worried you so, girls, Marcus," said Bardrick, shaking off his coat. "After we finished work at the castle, all the menfolk went to look for a lad who went missing, Fenris Kenhelm."

"Did you find him?" asked Fiona, concern rising in her as she remembered the shy lad of last night.

"Aye; or Fred Thorne did, at any rate. I didn't understand much of what he said when he came in dripping wet, but I think he found Fenris injured and came back to fetch help. So several of the men set out to bring him in, and the rest of us went home." He shrugged, seating himself at the table and shutting his eyes. "I don't doubt we will hear more tomorrow."

"Injured how?" called Marcus.

Bardrick's eyes opened and squinted in irritation towards his voice. "I do not know. Peony, have you anything to eat? I'm quite hungry."

"Of course!" Peony's silky-lashed eyes opened wide in dismay. She set the last of supper's stew in front of Bardrick, and after a pause declared, "Well, I am off to bed. Fiona?"

"I will come," murmured Fiona. She silently watched Bardrick eat. "Is Fred Thorne all right?" she asked at last.

Bardrick looked up in surprise.

"I heard you say he was wet. What happened?"

He shrugged. "He must have fallen in a creek. I don't know how he is, but I daresay he will be well enough as long as he gets warm again."

Fiona sat quietly with her hands clasped in her lap, the thoughts spinning in her head, full of worry and uncertainty. She and her family were safe and whole this night . . . but others were not.

~

The firelight shone dimly on the slight figure beside its dying flames, who was alone in the room save for the young man leaning over him.

"Why will you not wake?" Mordred whispered, laying an imploring hand on the bandage wound awkwardly over one side of Fenris' face. He caught his brother's hands in his and pressed his forehead against them. "Answer me, Fenris, please . . . "

As if in reply, Fenris' fingers stirred. Mordred tightened his grip, bitter tears threatening to break the surface. If he had not—

The hand shifted in his again. Fenris twitched slightly, and a murmuring noise escaped his lips as he moved with increasing restlessness.

"Fenris," Mordred begged, scanning his brother's taut features.

Fenris' eyes opened slowly and met his. "Mord-red," he said with an effort.

"Fenris? How is it? Can you hear me?"

"Mordred—my head hurts, so much—it's blinding—I can hardly see you." His voice stuttered and broke, and he shut his eyes tightly, his face creasing in agony.

"Fenris," Mordred began. His own voice failed, and he started again, very gently. "Fenris, it will be all right. I promise. Are you cold?"

His eyes opened again, hazy with pain. "No . . . I feel hot, Mordred."

Mordred touched Fenris' forehead with sinking heart and felt the warmth radiating from it.

Fenris struggled to keep his eyes open. "Mordred, don't leave—"

"I'm here, Fenris."

"Don't leave, please," Fenris repeated. His eyes were looking through Mordred, wandering.

"I am not leaving, Fenris." Mordred took his brother's burning hands and held them fiercely.

CHAPTER THREE

MORDRED WOKE TO A HAND on his shoulder. He sat up, pushing it away, bewildered.

"It is morning," said Braegon.

"What happened?"

Braegon looked at him. "What happened? Laufeia says she dozed off in Mirda's room and came out to find you fast asleep next to Fenris. We put a blanket over you and let you sleep."

"How is Fenris?" Mordred looked over towards the fireplace.

"He has been delirious all night." Braegon raked his fingers through his hair. "I do not know what to do; maybe Mr. Earle can help somehow."

Mordred threw the blanket aside and stood, turning toward Fenris. Laufeia was sitting beside him with a wet cloth held against his forehead. His thin cheeks were flushed hotly, his dark hair wet. His eyes were shut, but he tossed constantly and cried out at intervals.

"We must leave soon," said Braegon quietly behind Mordred. "Come, have some breakfast first."

At the thought of eating, Mordred's stomach turned. "Never mind that," he said. "Let us go now."

"Mordred," said Braegon, his features adamant yet distressed. "You cannot work all day on an empty stomach."

"I do not want any food," said Mordred roughly, turning away.

Braegon's shoulders lifted slightly. "Well, you will at least wait for me, for I have not eaten either." He went to the table. After a long moment Mordred followed him and forced several mouthfuls of the cooked meal down. They stepped out shortly into the sharp winter air. Mordred had not known how stifling the house was until he felt the clean, stinging coldness in his lungs. The wind blew freshly on his face, and the sun, though hidden, lent a peaceful whiteness to the thin clouds concealing it.

Mordred felt estranged from it all. It was full of hope and refused to grieve with him.

But why would he deserve grief? It was his fault that—

"What of Fred?" he asked aloud to halt the terrible thought.

"He was a touch feverish during the night, but around dawn he slept, and when he woke, he insisted that he was fine. He and Daren left shortly before you got up. I doubt we will see him at the castle, though," he added.

Mordred was scarcely listening by the end. He did not care, not really. All he could see was the darkened room he had left behind, and the bright spot of Laufeia's hair next to Fenris' restless body.

They walked under the castle gates, and Braegon sped across to Mr. Earle to exchange anxious words with him. Left alone, Mordred looked around and saw the foreman making for him.

He looked angry, and Mordred knew he had not forgiven him for their argument yesterday. "Kenhelm!" he bellowed. "Where's your brat of a brother? Did you ever find him?"

Mordred held in his anger and cocked one eyebrow coolly. "Thank you, sir, yes."

The man bristled at the mock courtesy in his tone. "Then where is he? Dead?"

Mordred's cold front grew still colder. "No, sir."

Before he could continue further, Mr. Earle came between them. "Fenris Kenhelm is ill today," he interposed, his patient face steady and calming. "He will not be coming for some time."

"To lose all my crew, am I?" the foreman grumbled. He swung back on Mordred. "All right, then, you can go over there with Kenneth Denholm and help fitting the stones."

"Certainly." With the barest dip of his head, Mordred turned and walked scornfully away.

~

"Daren!" Kenneth hailed the other man. "How is Fred?"

"He is doing well, at least it seems so," answered Daren, pausing in his route for the rubble carts. "But he was quite tired out when we arrived at the house and the girls agreed that he should not come to work."

"A wetting in winter is not to be taken lightly," agreed Kenneth. "He'll do well to rest a day or two."

Daren nodded. "And what of you and Jerithan?"

Kenneth smiled wryly. "We are all right."

"It cannot be easy raising a child on your own," said Daren.

"And a brother besides," said Kenneth with a sigh. "I look forward to the day when I take my bride under the roof and she can mother him. Marianne is always telling me I am too stern with him, and I don't doubt that she is right."

"A boy needs both," said Daren, smiling. "You and Marianne will make a fine couple, to be sure."

He went on with a farewell wave, and Kenneth set himself to the work of levering the shaped, sanded stones onto the wall in front of him.

"Hello," he said companionably as a shadow fell across him. A moment later, he saw with surprise that it was Mordred Kenhelm. "Hello," he said again, with less enthusiasm.

Mordred said nothing but heaved up one of the stones and set it down with a careful, decisive crack.

Kenneth followed suit, debating what to do next. It was in his nature to talk, but he was not sure that Mordred wanted to talk. At last he said the thing uppermost in his mind: "I hope your brother was not badly hurt."

"Hope away," Mordred said curtly, biting the words off. "It will change nothing."

Kenneth gave up.

~

Braegon came to Mordred's side as the evening light fell and the men in the castle dispersed. "Come with me."

"What?" Mordred asked, hearing the purpose in his voice. "Had Mr. Earle anything to say?"

"We are going to the Greys." Braegon walked quickly under the gates and struck out west over the clear ground by the lakeshore. "You have probably not heard of them."

"Who are they?" A curious sense of eagerness and danger stirred within him at Braegon's reserved tone.

"They are a strange family. They—" Braegon broke off, as though at a loss for words, and started again. "They have lived on this mountain for many decades, I understand, at least as long as the Earle and Stafford families. Some say they are related to the old lord of the place; in any case, they are rich, there is no question of that. But the singular thing is the curse, or gift, whatever it may be, that affects them."

"Go on," said Mordred as he fell silent.

"I do not know what began it, or where in their line—I doubt anyone does. Some say an ancestor wedded one of those who live undying." Again Braegon paused, and Mordred heard the reluctance to deal with what he did not understand.

"Whatever caused it, and whatever one calls it, it manifests itself in different ways. Some of the family are quite mad; some of them behave strangely, though they are sane enough. And some possess unnatural talents—one of the young boys can paint like a master artisan, and there are even rumors of vision-seers in other generations."

"Are they all afflicted by it?" Mordred questioned. "What of one who marries into them?"

"I do not think it can harm an outsider." Braegon ducked under a tree branch as they entered the woods again. "At least, I have seen Mrs. Grey, and she exhibits no peculiar trait. But no, in fact, not all their children display the curse. There are a few as ordinary as you and me. I have been told that if the father or mother is born unscathed, none of his offspring will inherit it either; but if he is afflicted, one cannot foresee the result."

"And why are we going there?"

"Because one of the Greys, the youngest daughter, can sense the ailments of people. And often, so says Mr. Earle, what to do for them."

They walked in silence until they broke out of the trees and onto a little trodden path, which wound up a rise towards the dark bulk of a large stone house. Lights gleamed invitingly in several windows, but as they passed through the iron gate that surrounded it, Mordred felt the closed-off air; this house was a seclusion, a place that one would not willingly enter.

Braegon led the way up to the imposing wall and wavered before the door with his hand half-raised. Somewhere inside the house a long, low laugh echoed, ending in a high-pitched giggle that sounded curiously out of control.

Braegon's knuckles fell against the wood, a penetrating sound that echoed in Mordred's ears. A short while later muffled footsteps approached, and the door swung inwards on a stream of golden light and a girl of about sixteen, Laufeia's age.

Her dark hair hung about her shoulders in a soft, heavy cloud. She was small and delicate as a finch, but the pretty cast of her face vanished under the cold imprint of cynicism in every feature.

She twitched one shoulder up brusquely. "Yes?"

"Irene Grey?" said Braegon.

"I am she. Why are you here?"

"His brother is ill; we thought you could help?"

"That depends," she answered, and turning, she called into the passage beyond, "Mother, I'm leaving."

"All right, dear!" came a distant reply. "Where?"

"I don't know, Mother. Goodbye." She jerked a red wool cape from a peg beside her and settled it around her shoulders.

"Irene!" came another voice from the hall, and a young man of twenty, with the same soft black hair, stepped into the light. "What is it?"

"Seems I'm wanted," returned Irene shortly.

Her brother looked, his brow creasing doubtfully as he saw their dim figures. "When will you be back?"

Irene shrugged in answer, wheeled, and shut the door briskly behind her.

“That was Therelane,” Braegon said in an undertone to Mordred as they started back down the path. “He is one of the unaffected Greys. He comes by the castle occasionally.”

“He is a rather discontented daydreamer and a time-waster,” sniffed Irene.

Startled into silence by the unexpected commentary, Braegon said no more.

“When did it happen?” Irene asked abruptly when they were halfway to the house.

“Last night,” answered Braegon. “He was in the wilds and some animal attacked him.”

“Ah.”

And they were quiet again.

“We must be near,” Irene observed sometime later.

“Aye,” said Braegon. “There is the house. You . . . felt something?”

For reply, Irene gave him a palpably irritated silence. She swept ahead of them to the door and stalked in.

When Mordred entered after her, she stood already by Fenris, who lay beside the fire no different than they had left him. Laufeia and Mirda were staring in surprise.

“Well?” Mordred asked at last, unable to keep back his impatience as she surveyed Fenris with folded arms.

Irene’s head snapped up, and she returned his stare evenly. “I don’t know what you’re expecting, young man. I’m not a magician, so don’t expect me to come out with an instant cure for cold and fever.”

“Are you saying there is nothing you can do?” Mordred demanded.

“Goodness. Yes, I can do nothing. However, you can try to bring down his fever. Have you feverfew? Willow bark? There must be some wife in this town who could give you that, and it will help if you apply it diligently. Other than that, you'll have to wait it out. As for his wound, it hasn't gone bad yet. You might see if you can get comfrey, too, and put a poultice on that, for if it gets inflamed, he's likely done for, by the state he's in."

"Feverfew; willow bark; comfrey," repeated Braegon. "Mirda can ask for them from Mrs. Earle tomorrow."

"There you are." Irene turned. Her cape spun and flapped behind her out the door.

~

"How was work today?" asked Peony brightly as Bardrick sat down to supper with them. "Any news of the missing boy?"

"They got him back to the Kings' all right, from what I heard," answered Bardrick. "But he was hurt."

"We knew that," said Marcus.

"Yes," said Bardrick with mild exasperation. "He got a bad wound in his head. Braegon said something must have been trying to claw at him. When they left, he was out of his mind with delirium."

"Poor Fenris," said Peony, her eyes softening in sympathy.

"Poor Mordred," Fiona murmured. A memory had flashed suddenly to the surface of her mind, the memory of standing beside Fred Thorne on the wedding night, and the infinitely tender way in which Mordred had spoken his brother's name: *"Fenris."*

"What was that?" Peony said, looking at her.

Fiona had been only half-conscious of speaking aloud. "Mordred," she replied slowly. "I—never mind." 'Twas hard to explain, at least to Peony, the quick intuition that led her to read so easily the thoughts and actions of others.

"Is your ankle feeling any better, Marcus?" Peony's solicitous query turned the general attention from the Kenhelms.

Marcus sent his eyes rolling back dramatically in his head. "In all my sixteen years I've never felt such agony," he moaned.

Peony sprang up, looking alarmed.

Marcus sputtered. "Sit down! It's fine. It never felt better. I can hardly believe my misfortune. Two sisters, and one can't take teasing, while the other doesn't even understand it!"

Fiona got up herself with a small sigh. "What was that you were saying before dinner about the Thorne family, Peony?"

"I was thinking to pay them a visit in a few days. Did you want to accompany me?"

"I will," answered Fiona after a moment. She did not know whether she wanted to. Aye, she could find delight in it. But there was still a faint ache inside her, an ache of loneliness. She wanted another mind to open to hers, to speak and listen, to do the things that had delighted her when she had still been Lady Fiona in the halls of Segelas.

Those things are gone now. It is no use to wish for them.

No. The ache within her grew. *But I wish for them all the same.*

~

The fire flickered with a sickening sameness over the room where Fenris slept fitfully, the two beside him keeping ever constant watch.

Laufeia stroked the damp hair back from Fenris' hot forehead and looked to Mordred, whose lips were closed into a taut line that mirrored the stifled torment in his eyes.

"Mordred," she said, "tell me how it all happened."

"I argued with the foreman," he said dully. "I sent Fenris away and told him to come back in a short time. I ended by arguing with the man for near an hour. When it was over, Fenris had not returned, and when I waited for another hour he still did not. Braegon and I went out to look for him, and when the workday was done the other men came to help. That is all there is to tell."

It took a moment for the full meaning of his words to settle in Laufeia's mind. *"I sent Fenris away . . . "*

With a sudden, piercing pain, she saw the full measure of his suffering, and tears filled her eyes as she lowered them. *After thinking he has failed him for so long, now—this?*

CHAPTER FOUR

FRED SET HIS BOWL DOWN and stood up. "You are ready to go, Daren?"

Daren nodded and opened the door, waving to the girls still gathered at the table. Coming towards him, Fred bent briefly with a cough.

Isabelle leaped up. "Fred! You mustn't."

Sandy snorted. "Isabelle . . . "

"Sister," Fred answered patiently, "it is sillier for me to stay away from work when I am all but recovered."

"But, Fred, you coughed!"

He stepped out the door. "I will take it easy on the way, Isabelle. Farewell!"

He walked slowly down the whitened road, lagging behind Daren a short way and delighting in the spangles of light that the sun struck across the crusted snow: shifting sparks, silver and blue and red-gold. As he passed a thatch-roofed house, he saw the slim girl's figure bent over an old well and paused, observing her lift the bucket out and start back to the cottage. Her bright head shone like a star of gold in the clear light. Then she saw him watching and set the bucket down, coming swiftly.

"Aye? Did you need anything?"

He shook his head. "Nay. My lady Fiona?"

"Aye," she acknowledged softly, lowering her eyes. "It is good to meet you again, Fred Thorne."

"And you, my lady."

She lifted her head and met his eyes, the movement shy but graceful. "I am glad to see you well. I was told how you fell in a creek while searching for the Kenhelm lad."

"It happened after I had found him, but yes." He smiled ruefully. "'Twas a rather foolish thing in all, I fear; for I tried to jump the brook in my haste, instead of trying to find a way to circumvent it."

A cleft of thought drew itself between her light brows. Her small, proud head lifted with quick decisiveness, a sudden ardency animating her face. "Foolish, maybe," she answered, "but maybe not. Who knows how long it might have taken you to find another way?"

"We do not know that it would have taken long," he pointed out in answer.

Again her eyes lit, and she drew an eager breath. "That is true, we do not know. Therefore, there was naught to choose between them, and the one you took proved well for Fenris."

Fred's soft smile touched his lips. "I see we shall have to leave the bulk of such a discussion for another time. You are a maid of quick intelligence, and doubtlessly skilled in art of argument and persuasion; but I have work at the castle and must take my leave."

She laughed faintly. "Indeed, you flatter me now."

"Nay! I did not mean it as flattery, my lady Fiona. Have I not spoken with you before now, to form a knowledge of your intellect? Understand that what I have said to you, I mean in truth that it is so. Farewell." He raised his hand in a parting gesture and turned towards the road.

~

Fiona pressed one hand to her hot cheek and the other to her heart, which was leaping with warm thrills of pleasure. It was unsettling to be so complimented—and by one who was almost a stranger. 'Twas something Bardrick might have said to her— Bardrick who had known her from birth. Another man would not have said it, or if he did would not have meant it.

"But he is not like other men," she whispered, and startled herself with its truth. "He is not like other men. He did mean it."

"Fiona! Do you mean to stand out there all day? Who was that?" called Peony all in a breath from the doorway.

"I'm sorry, Peony. That was Fred Thorne," answered Fiona, coming quickly into the kitchen.

"Fred Thorne," Peony mused. "Now is that the handsome dark-haired man whom I met nearby the Earles' yesterday?"

"You must mean his brother Daren; Fred has much lighter hair. He is the one who found Fenris Kenhelm."

"Ah! Yes, I remember now, it was Daren. So, are they much alike?"

"I—" Fiona hesitated, wondering. For their features were not so similar; Daren's as she remembered them were finer, more cleanly drawn, his face slightly narrower than his brother's. Their color of hair and eye differed. But the way they walked and bore themselves was so alike . . .

"I think they are," she answered. "Though they may not look it at first."

"Whatever that means!" sighed Peony. "But that is nice, that you have a friend."

"Yes," said Fiona after a moment, very slowly. "Yes, I suppose that is true."

She stood quietly, taking in the revelation as it expanded and filled her with a pure, glad buoyancy that lifted her heart on singing wings.

She had—a friend.

~

Laufeia poured the dark, bitter tea between Fenris' cracked lips. He choked faintly on the liquid, and then swallowed. When the cup was drained, she sat back and looked at him. He was no different than before, tossing in weak movements on the pallet, murmuring incoherently.

"It must take a little time to do anything," said Mirda gently beside her.

"Yes," Laufeia agreed reluctantly. She rose to help Mirda with the small chores of the house.

She gave him the tea twice again that day but could not discern any change in him. Her heart sank each time she looked over at the fire and saw the helpless figure that looked thinner and weaker every time. The fever was taking over, ravaging his exhausted body. The bones stuck sharply out of his face; his cheeks were hectically flushed.

At evening they ate in silence in Mirda's bedchamber, for Laufeia could not bear to touch food in that awful room. The young men had not yet returned.

The fire was sinking when she entered the room again and sat down beside Fenris. He lay still, his chest lifting in faint, panting breaths, his eyes open.

"Laufeia," he said.

She started.

"Laufeia?" he repeated weakly, his quiet grey eyes studying her in a question. His forehead was wet, but cool to the touch.

"Fenris! When—oh, Fenris. Is your head hurting you much?"

"It hurts," he said, "but not so much anymore." He moved his arm, reaching up perplexedly to touch the bandage.

"It happened a few days ago. Do you remember?"

"There were so many dreams," he said, his voice weary, "I don't know what was a dream. I remember being hot for so long, and I was tired but couldn't sleep. And my whole head hurt. But now it is just one place."

"It looks like you were clawed by something," she told him and saw his eyes widen. "Can you remember that now?"

"Yes," he said softly. "It was a bear. I don't know what roused it, but it came up on me all at once. I ran all through the trees, but it was so quick, and no matter where I went, it was right behind me. I didn't know what to do, and finally I turned, to try to run past and confuse it. And I think it was swinging at me then, because I felt something scrape up my forehead, very hard and fast. It made everything go black for a moment, and suddenly I was falling. I don't remember hitting the ground, just lying there trying to catch my breath, and then it was all black again."

He was quiet for a little, his eyes drifting over the room. Then he stirred. "Where is Mordred?"

Laufeia looked at him. But before she could answer the outer door opened, and the cold wind blew in as Mordred's figure entered with a tired step.

"Mordred!" she said quickly, rising.

Mordred looked from her to Fenris and a choked sound escaped him. He came across the room in a long stride.

As Laufeia watched him embrace Fenris, the first relief ebbed away into something duller, and an old Rehirnish proverb came to her mind: *Te adda rine bocca murat, tu adda rine lech.*

"To climb down is easier than to climb up."

~

The next morning was bright, the sun ablaze with a heat to set droplets sliding down the icicles. Fenris' wound, to Laufeia's delight, was all but closed on its own. With Mirda's help she removed the stitches from it, and then propped Fenris against the wall with blankets and pallet so that he could sit up but still rest.

"Now that Fenris is improving," said Braegon as they breakfasted, "you will probably be wanting to move into your own house."

"Certainly," said Laufeia, answering his smile. "I am sorry; it must have been quite crowded for you these past days."

Braegon laughed and would have spoken again, but the door opened, and a young man stood on the threshold. "Braegon?" he called.

"Kenneth!" Braegon stood. "What did you need?"

"Naught." Kenneth smiled foolishly and started again. "It's just I was passing, and I thought I might mention that Marianne and I are to marry on the fifteenth, the midwinter festival."

Braegon laughed aloud. "I could not wait to share such news in your place either! Congratulations, my friend. Two weddings in a month, in winter at that."

Kenneth chuckled, and glanced down, catching sight of Fenris and the bold, red mark on his pale forehead. Fenris met his gaze for a second, eyes widening, and then he dropped them with a quick shudder. An unconscious stillness fell over the room.

Kenneth looked quickly away and waved to Braegon. "Farewell!" he called and walked out.

The silence lingered on for a moment or two; then Braegon resumed, "As we were saying—"

"Yes," said Mordred harshly, moving away from the window where he had been standing. "Let us impose on your generosity no longer."

"Mordred," breathed Laufeia. "What—"

"I daresay you have long been desiring our absence already," he went on, cold, stiff.

"Mordred!" She leaped up and jerked him by his arm, leading him into the bedroom. "What was that for!" she demanded in a heated whisper. "How could you speak so?"

"How do you think, like them, to pass over what just happened?" he cried passionately. "Pretend it never was? Laufeia, do you not see what is ahead of us? Do you think that that scar is ever going to disappear? He will bear it for the rest of his life, Laufeia!"

She started at his words, shook her head, but they were true. She had half-realized it herself last night, had she not?

Mordred whirled away, his face white and hard as winter. The door slammed shut behind him.

~

Marcus limped gingerly around on his ankle. "Oh . . . I don't know."

"Stand up straight and walk like a normal person, Marcus," said Bardrick with his older-brotherly patience. "It might feel better that way."

Marcus shot him a look that said, "I am enjoying my status as invalid." But he straightened and put his foot carefully forward. With a faint shrug he took one step, and another.

"Well, I declare," he said with a grin. "It feels like I never sprained it." He picked up his coat. "Time to go. I admit, it's nice to walk oneself again. We'll see you tonight, girls!"

In the courtyard, Marcus glanced casually around. "Looks much the same," he remarked. "I can see there hasn't been much done while I was away."

"Marcus," Bardrick said with tired remonstrance. "Do not let the foreman hear you saying that."

"All right," said Marcus. "Is he in a bad mood?"

"He has been touchy for some time now . . . " Bardrick paused and did not finish his sentence.

"Who is that?" Marcus asked, waving at one of those nearby. "I don't remember seeing him before. Is he one of the Kenhelms?"

Bardrick cast a hurried glance Mordred's way. "Yes," he muttered. "And Marcus, I would not talk to him and definitely not make your jokes around him."

"Not talk to him? But what if I am curious about things like—"

"All right, Marcus! I forbid you to go near him."

"Kenhelm!" the foreman shouted over the courtyard. Marcus heard the undisguised anger in his tone. "Over there and start helping with the shaping!"

Mordred gave a cool nod, wheeling away with shoulders taut and head high.

Marcus raised one eyebrow at Bardrick. Bardrick said nothing, but tugged Marcus firmly behind him to their own post.

"Do you not like him so much?" Marcus asked, referring to Mordred.

"I don't dislike him, Marcus," said Bardrick.

But Marcus could read people as intuitively as Fiona could. The exasperation in his brother's tone was too forced, closer to annoyance. "You don't exactly dislike him, maybe, but you don't like him either, do you?" He cocked his head and studied Bardrick.

Bardrick's countenance pled understanding from Marcus as he justified himself. "He is not—enjoyable to be around. It was understandable while his brother was ill, but we heard yesterday morning that Fenris is doing better. And he is still as cold, as distant as ever." Bardrick shrugged. "How is one expected to like the company of a man who acts as haughty as Steward Froeda? I do not act like a lord around these folk, and we are in fact of noble blood; I count myself as one of them. Why cannot he do the same?"

"He sounds intriguing," said Marcus with a certain excitement. "Forgive me, Bardrick," he added, catching the look on his older brother's face. "I suppose he is quite irksome. But you must see, from an impersonal point of view—"

"Aye," snorted Bardrick. "I daresay for a scholar he would make an interesting study in human arrogance."

Marcus sputtered with laughter.

~

Laufeia looked around the dark little room, thinking of the happy spirit that had filled her the last time she stood in it. Now a dull, tired feeling sank into her. Slowly, she walked forward to light the fire.

Fenris lay beside the door with his head pillowed on his arms, his eyes closed. Though she and Mirda had supported him the whole way, the walk of one mile had utterly exhausted him. She thought to help him to his bed, but after a moment's consideration laid a blanket over him and hoped he would rest well.

Mordred came late, and Laufeia had begun to worry that he was lost trying to find their house before he finally entered, stamping snow from his boots.

"How did the work fare?" she asked, hoping to be cheerful for his sake. "Did you accomplish much?"

"What would I know of that?" he shot back. "The foreman does not share his counsels with me." He jerked a chair up and slammed it down by the table.

"Mordred, hush!" she snapped, dropping her voice to an angry whisper and looking pointedly to the corner where Fenris lay.

"Oh?" he said, his lips thinning in annoyance. "Now it is everyone's duty to order me."

"You've wakened Fenris," she answered heatedly.

Mordred's voice lowered. "Well, if you had told me why you wanted me to stop shouting—"

"I shouldn't have to give you a reason!" she cried, thoroughly vexed. "Besides, it was your first outburst that woke him, before I said anything to you at all. Why don't you just try behaving yourself?"

"Behaving myself? What is Fenris doing lying on the floor when he ought to be resting on the pitiful excuse we have for a bed?"

"Mordred, if you begin attacking the generosity of everything these kind people have given us, I will—I will scream!"

"Much good that will do," he retorted scathingly.

"I'll throw your own straw tick out the window! You might feel a bit more gratitude when you don't have anything to sleep on anymore. As for Fenris on the floor, I would like to see you force him up when he can scarcely stand from exhaustion!"

"Leave Fenris out of this."

"Mordred Kenhelm, you brought him into—"

But before she had finished her sentence, Mordred kicked his chair back violently and walked out of the room.

~

The small, diamond-paned windows let tired winter's daylight into the long room where the busy women had gathered. Almost all Ceristen's wives and daughters had come to the Earles' house to help young Marianne prepare for her wedding. Wood clacked lightly on wood on the northern side, where the older women set themselves to knitting a colorful woolen quilt. Marjorie Delaney was among them, her countenance sweet and staid save for any mention of Charles' name, whereupon she blushed and focused her eyes more firmly on her work.

From the second knot much laughter and talking resounded, for they were constructing Marianne's wedding dress, and thither most of the younger girls gravitated.

Only Sandy could not seem to decide which group to settle on. She wandered back and forth between them, now picking up a woolen ball and needles, then a handful of blue linen and the shears.

"I shall marry in silk," said Linda Boccin dreamily, her black braid slipping over one shoulder as she whipped the yellow flax thread in and out across the bodice.

Mirda giggled. "How on earth?"

"Why, that is easy." Linda tossed her head, cheeks glowing pink with fervor. "I must simply marry a very rich man. I'm sure there's one who would have me."

"Hah!" Lia Earle, Marianne's fifteen-year-old sister, fluttered her lashes over captivating green eyes. "I'd rather have a handsome husband than a rich one."

"Yes," agreed Samantha slyly, knotting her dark curls up on the back of her head. The eldest of the Earle sisters, she had married Julius Mogra last fall. She leaned forward. "And Kenneth is very handsome."

Marianne's pale face erupted into redness that shamed her hair, and her laughter mingled with the others around her.

Sandy rolled her eyes and sauntered back to the knitting.

"It turned out for the best, if I do say so myself." Mrs. Earle nodded happily. Her once-dark hair was a washed-out grey, her green eyes faded, and her form undeniably plump. But in the pretty tilt of her head and her long lashes were reminders of her three daughters' beauty. "And Arad—oh, I've run out of yarn. Kirade, would you? There, thank you." She accepted the hank of wool from Edrach Stafford's severe-faced wife. "Anyway, Arad says . . . "

Sandy groaned inwardly. Gossip, gossip, all froth and no broth.

Back at the wedding dress, the girls had diverted to the topic of handsome young men.

"Your brother is fairly handsome, Mirda," Linda Boccin said generously. "Braegon, that is; Filian is rather young still."

"I'm sure he doesn't care," said Mirda with a frank, laughing air. "Braegon is bound up in ideas of work, not courting."

Sandy looked at Cecelia, wondering what she thought of the conversation. But Cecelia's hazel eyes were fixed with customary composure on the cloth between her fingers, and her demure face gave no hint that she heard the discussion around her.

"Mordred Kenhelm is very handsome." Linda tittered softly.

Several of the other girls glanced at one another.

"Who's Mordred Kenhelm?" asked another carelessly. Sandy could not remember who she was—one of Mrs. Stafford's daughters, maybe.

"Don't you remember, Lagola?" said Linda in surprise. "He is the one who just came here, whose brother got lost in the Wilds. Your father was one of the people who helped look for the boy."

“Oh.” Lagola shrugged nonchalantly and pushed back the bright curls tumbling around her face. “I remember now. He was at Marjorie Delaney’s wedding, wasn’t he? But I didn’t see him.”

“He is so handsome, though,” Linda said, and blushed. Sandy could not help a snort.

“Oh, gracious,” said Lagola, her brown eyes dancing with mingled disgust and amusement. “How boring. I don’t care whether my husband is handsome; at least, not much. I want him to be fun. At any rate, I’ve no interest in marrying for a long time yet, and this is proving terribly dull.”

Lia Earle threw her pert voice in again. “Mordred Kenhelm may be handsome, but I’ve heard he isn’t very pleasant.”

“Lia!” said Marianne and Samantha reprovingly in the same breath.

Lia’s face reddened. “That’s what Kenneth says,” she protested. “He says that Mordred doesn’t speak kindly to anyone on the work crew and gets in fights with the foreman.”

The girls looked awkwardly at one another, and no one said anything.

Sandy watched with folded arms. She was thinking of ghosts out of the near past.

A guardhouse at the West Gate, and a harsh-voiced soldier named Captain Murray; a girl with an older brother— a stoic face, and a hurting heart.

Then Mirda stood up, scattering bits of white and blue linen over the floor. “He speaks well to Braegon,” she said, her clear blue eyes filled with rebuke. “I do not know all they have borne, but it is more than any of us. You cannot condemn him, not before you know his side.”

Sandy studied Mirda in surprise as the girl sat down and picked up the scissors. *Thank you . . . That was what I wanted to say.*

CHAPTER FIVE

MORDRED LEANED ON THE ICY wall as the foreman barked out the noon break. When he saw the shadow coming towards him and heard Braegon's familiar clipped gait, he shifted subtly away so that he could not face the other young man.

"How goes it, Mordred?" The simple question was quiet the way Braegon uttered it, gentle yet probing with deep understanding and concern.

Mordred tried to give a soft answer in return. But he saw Fenris' white, tired face with that irrevocable dark line scoring across it, and a tight, lashing anger built stubbornly in his chest. "What is it to you?" he snapped.

Braegon did not leave; instead, in a gesture of forgiveness, he held out his cup and waited for Mordred to share a draught from it.

The anger would not stop, knotting itself up through his throat in painful, strangling cords. He slapped the cup away that Braegon was holding out to him, hurling it to the ground. The warmed ale pooled hissing on the frozen stone.

Mordred wheeled and stared at his feet, shaking, sharply aware as Braegon bent to pick up the cup, turned, and walked away. When the memory stopped playing in a cruel circle through his head, he stirred himself and opened the parcel that Laufeia had made for his dinner.

The sight of the food did nothing but sicken him and incite a stirring of the anger. He could not bear to eat with the faces dancing in his head, taunting him, first Fenris', now Braegon's.

Mordred flung the little bundle away into a snowdrift by the wall and walked with a swift, lithe stride across the courtyard and out the gate. Let none of them approach him and ask why he was not eating, as though they cared. As though his welfare were a matter of concern to anyone but himself.

The peacefulness of the silent road and the cold air steadied him. The tight, raging storm slipped loose from its moorings, ebbing away somewhere deep inside, and he walked on with a step free and graceful, his head uplift and his eyes roving the hills.

At first, he did not see the house, nor the thin trail leading up to it. He saw only a crippled rabbit, some fox's almost-prey hobbling under the trees, and instantly his hand was on the ground, feeling for a stone. He let fly with an ease of long practice, and his missile struck the animal's head squarely; the next minute Mordred was beside it and had wrung its neck. 'Twas not every day he had fresh meat laid in his way, but they would have a stew in their pot tonight.

Then he saw a path.

He straightened slowly, the dead rabbit in his arms. It opened onto the road, yes, but from there it had appeared only a gap between tree and tree, not worthy of any notice. At this angle he could see its twists through the thicket, an opening a little way beyond, and the dark wall of a house in the clearing there.

For a moment he stood, a quick curiosity brightening his grey eyes, an eagerness that slowly stirred to decision. He buttoned the rabbit inside his coat and walked unhesitatingly down the crooking trail.

The house was not like the cottages of the village. It was built in a strange arching style, all of dark wood, and did not follow a uniform plan; wings pushed out in odd places, as did smaller rooms, little nubbing things that seemed desirous to engulf the land about. A high peak pushed black against the whitish sky. Intricate engravings lay all over, the work of long years, maybe generations, for there was scarce an inch of wood that was left untouched; and these Mordred liked the less as he came near, yet he could not have said why, for they were lovely.

He wandered about it for several long minutes, attracted by the strangeness of it, longing to know its secrets. Then to his ears, faint but startling, came the call of the horn that signaled the end of noon.

Mordred whirled. He gawked foolishly at strange black houses and then he ran swiftly through the woods, out onto the beaten road, and back toward the distant walls of the castle. When he arrived, no one remarked on his absence, and the foreman did not seem to have been aware of it—a fact which Mordred suspected he had Braegon to thank for. But he had no chance to speak to him the rest of that day, and he wondered whether Braegon were behind that, too.

~

There was something rested about Mordred when he came home that night—the way he walked, the way his shoulders swung easily with his gait. Laufeia wondered at it and watched him closely all evening. He was not happy, she could not say that; but something had drawn him out of his cold, brooding shell, something had diverted his mind. When he took off his coat, a dead rabbit fell out onto the floor, but he did not even notice until she indicated it with some asperity.

"Oh, yes," said Mordred absently. "There was a rabbit." Like an afterthought, he added, "You can cook it."

She could scarcely get his attention to address him, much less ask him what had happened. He did not react to his name, nor speak once through dinner. His eyes narrowed thoughtfully in intense reverie.

What could have caused this change, Laufeia did not know, but she was not at all sure she liked it.

She need not have worried. By morning, the unknown distraction had lost its charm. Mordred was as bitterly brooding as he ever had been, and he would scarcely eat, but left for the castle a lean, weary figure whose shoulders sagged in a despondency that made her heart ache to see.

~

"Fiona, come," called Peony from the kitchen. "Isabelle Thorne gave us a loaf of bread yesterday, and I'm dropping by her house to return the favor with a meat pie."

"Why not the bread?" Fiona queried with a gesture to the loaves that Peony and she had shaped and baked that morning. "If that is what she gave us?"

Peony shook her head with a frown. "No, Fiona, it doesn't do to give the same thing. It might seem like I was showing off my own skills as better than hers."

"I see." Fiona dropped her eyes, running her fingers lightly over the rounded loaf nearest her. She had been too young all those years ago, a tangle-headed child not long weaned, mastering letters and conduct, not the delicate framework of customs and social graces that Peony remembered. Now that those things were a part of their lives once more, she must learn from Peony how not to shame herself in an artless moment.

"So, are you ready?" said Peony, donning a cape and reaching for the latch.

"What do you mean?"

Peony turned back in surprise. "Are you not coming to the Thornes? I thought you wished to accompany me."

Flustered warmth rushed to Fiona's face as she recalled her promise several nights before. "I—I don't—Peony, I—"

"Fiona," said Peony, quite kindly, "you mustn't stammer so. You know better." She paused. "If you would rather stay, that's all right."

Rather stay? No. Her heart shrank from the idea of a morning alone and dreary in the silent house. Yet the proposal of engaging with people had caught her unawares; she felt stranded, afraid. How could one desire and dread the same thing so strongly? Was something amiss with her—was she cursed?

You must put a stop to your childish behavior. Only your rearing in seclusion handicaps you so.

"I shall come," she said to Peony, her submissive tone entirely different from the stern voice she chastised herself within.

~

Isabelle Thorne greeted them at the door. Shorter than either of them, dark hair piled high on her head, a full but not stout figure. "Good morning," she said pleasantly. "Peony Segelas, is it not?"

"Indeed, and my sister Fiona as well," answered Peony. "I have a little gift for you in return for yours to us yesterday."

"Oh, thank you!" exclaimed Isabelle and accepted the bundle graciously. "Now come in," she invited, "and sit down awhile."

How alike they were, mused Fiona, Peony and this Isabelle Thorne. Kind; sociable; eager hostesses. Perhaps Isabelle, too, was careful with the household accounts and sensitive to any hint of impropriety.

"Sandra," said Isabelle as she led them into the little living-room, "and Cecelia, and Gwenda."

The one she had dubbed Sandra squirmed and flushed slightly on her fair cheekbones. "Sandy," she muttered in protest.

"Well, yes," said Isabelle, laughing, "we all call her Sandy."

Cecelia was Isabelle's height but slimmer, and fair in coloring like Fred. She studied them with a grave, remarkably aloof face, saying nothing, and Fiona met her gaze with startling ease. Here was one she could hold her own to. Here was another woman who observed first, and then made judgment.

As for Gwenda—

"I have seen Gwenda before," she said.

"Oh?" said Isabelle, raising her brows in question.

"At your sister's wedding, was it not? Marjorie's? I may have seen you as well," she added, "but I think that most of you were dancing, for your brother Fred said it was a pity he could not introduce us to one another."

"So you were at the wedding! What a pity we did not meet! And you spoke with Fred?" Isabelle posed the question with a degree of curiosity.

"Yes, I did." Fiona wished that the memory of Marcus' teasing had not surfaced, else maybe color would not have so mortifyingly tinged her cheeks.

A proud smile tilted Isabelle's lips. "He is a good man, is he not?"

"He is," said Fiona honestly. "He is one of the gentlest, kindest men I have ever known."

"Is he the eldest of you?" put in Peony.

"Aye," Isabelle said. "It is strange, I confess, to have an elder brother . . . I had grown quite used to being the eldest myself before we were reunited."

"Once, then, you were separated?" Peony queried. "But how?"

"Now, that is quite the tale!" said Isabelle and laughed. "You will have to ask Fred for it in full sometime. In fact, I should invite you to sup with us at some appropriate evening. After Marianne and, what's-his-name?"

"Kenneth," supplied Sandy glibly from her sprawled position in front of the fireplace.

"Kenneth, yes. Their wedding falls on the midwinter festival —what a fine holiday we shall make of it!— and sometime after that, you must visit; and then you may see the whole family, and we yours!"

"It is a wonderful idea," said Peony brightly.

Then she and Isabelle fell into a busy conversation of nothings and little particulars, and Fiona glanced to Cecelia.

Cecelia returned her steady look. "Well met, Fiona," she said with an unexpected smile that warmed her austere countenance.

"And you," answered Fiona simply.

Silence, unhurried and serene, hung between them.

"Your smile is like your brother's," said Fiona thoughtfully. "He smiled at me so when he first saw my sadness the night of the wedding and sought me out."

"Is it so?" A wistful curiosity edged Cecelia's lilting tone. "I have never heard any say I am like him, and I often wonder."

"'Tis true, not all bear equal likeness, even from house to house," Fiona said with a smile of her own. "Some take Bardrick and Peony for husband and wife, not blood kin; whereas the Kenhelm family, 'twould be nigh impossible to mistake their relation."

"Yes." But Cecelia's voice dropped on the word, and her solemn gaze drifted into the distance, as though Fiona's words had sent her mind elsewhere altogether. "Fred," she murmured slowly, "Fred thinks that Mordred Kenhelm is suffering."

"Suffering!" Fiona was struck by the choice of word.

"Yes," said Cecelia, and there was no secret relish in the sadness of her words.

And Fiona saw very clear in her mind that young, proud face, and the name spoken with such strange gentleness: *"Fenris . . . "*

The visit played itself out, little further conversation passing between Fiona and Cecelia, though the cheery chatter from the elder girls murmured throughout the house for a long while.

"I hope," said Peony solicitously as they left the Thornes, "that you have enjoyed yourself a little, Fiona."

"I have," Fiona assented. But her mind had wandered far from their visit. She was thinking of the loaves of bread on their table, and of three hurting people in a little house.

~

Laufeia pushed the rag slowly up the surface of the wall. The warmish water squeezed out between her fingers. She felt so tired; it was not that the housework was too much, but rather that it seemed to have lost all meaning. What was the use of making the effort? What was the use of anything? She watched the drips trickle down her hand in the dim light until they hung on the curve of her wrist, tawdry-grey globes that splatted with the tiniest of noises on the floor.

She turned to glance at Fenris, who looked back listlessly, a blanket over his knees. With a slow, inevitable tug, her gaze shifted to the half-healed line tracing up his forehead.

He knew. His eyes dropped; his face turned away from her.

Mrs. Earle's daughter Marianne had come by yesterday, with some spare lye, to say politely that they were welcome to the wedding. She had seen Fenris—she could not have failed to see Fenris, Laufeia told herself fiercely, struggling to think the best of the young red-haired girl. Her stare had lasted until Fenris, to Laufeia's relief and misery, turned and fled the room. Marianne had come to herself then with an embarrassed look at Laufeia and attempted to make small talk. And she had seemed so embarrassed by their poverty. By everything in the house. Fenris lived in a daze the rest of the day, and Mordred, when he came home, had of course asked what had upset Fenris—

Why, Fenris? She whirled and scrubbed the wet rag vehemently against the wall. *Why you? Why not anybody else?*

That evening, Mordred came home early.

"What happened?" Laufeia demanded at once, only to face her brother's most impassive expression as he kicked a chair out from the table and sat down.

She pressed him over and over, her anxiety growing, until he dropped his stony silence with a small, haughty, dismissive toss of the head. "A dispute with the foreman. He ordered me out of the courtyard and that was the end of it."

Laufeia's mouth fell agape.

"It is nothing," he snapped.

"Nothing!"

Mordred slapped both hands against the wood of the table. "I said, that was an end of it! He only sent me away for the evening; 'tis not as if I am fired. I will go back tomorrow, and all will proceed as usual. Am I so untrustworthy, then?" he added hotly as she leveled her most skeptical stare at him.

Laufeia refused to give him another response—she refused to heap more fuel on the quarrel she knew that he wanted. She turned around and marched out of the kitchen, leaving Mordred cross at the table and the stew-broth she had begun to prepare cold in the pot with no fire under it. The window-latch in the living-room was loose; she gave it a push and let the frigid breeze of winter's twilight brush her cheeks.

Something moved out in the blue-black shadows, a person's shape walking down the road.

"Oh, no. No."

"No what?" Mordred shouted, leaping up from the table and tearing into the room.

She whirled. "Nothing. Did my tone alarm you that much?"

"You sounded," Mordred shot back, "like there was something very wrong."

"Nothing is wrong."

"Then what did you squeal for?"

"Squeal! Mordred, I scarcely raised my voice, and you are treating this whole matter as far more significant than it is!"

"It is quite significant when my sister spouts 'no' sounding like the absolute end of the world is—"

"I want you to be quiet for a moment and listen to me!"

"Why did you groan like that?"

Laufeia stared at him, silent. She did not want to tell him. Let them squabble like children, but if he knew, it would change at once . . .

She lowered her eyes and quietly, pleadingly, answered his question. "Someone is coming to the house."

Mordred was no longer a childish brother flinging insults at her. He was a man, white-lipped with anger. "What!" he exploded. "What do these people want? What do they think they are doing here?"

She tried to hush him, but the anger had been building up inside him so long, and there was nowhere for it to go but out. "I will not stand for it. What can they gain by coming here? How many more of them want to stop by to gloat over our misfortunes? Commiserate about Fenris' injury while ogling his face? Do you realize what this is doing to Fenris? Do you realize—"

She seized his wrist and closed her own small fingers so tightly around it that he broke off with a sharp gasp.

"Mordred, enough. Enough! I—I don't want anyone here either." Her voice broke a little, and she swallowed back the tears prickling the corners of her eyes. Part of her was still angry at Mordred, but the other part knew that he was hurting, hurting more than she was. "Please, I don't know who this person is, but please be civil. Or go somewhere else if you cannot. We have to make do the best we can." She put up a hand to blot back the trail seeping down her cheek and moved toward the door.

"Laufeia," Mordred said huskily, his eyes soft, his voice rough and strained. "Laufeia, I'm sorry." He reached out, as though to touch the tears.

She turned her head, hiding them from his sight, knowing they had moved him more than the words she said. He pulled her close, only to let her go quickly as the knock sounded from without. Laufeia went to answer it.

Firelight from the kitchen streamed faintly out the door and illuminated the young woman on the threshold. She was tall, her hair under the shawl glimmering gold, her face slender and noble and filled with peace.

"Laufeia," she said. "I am Fiona Segelas."

Laufeia hesitated and nodded. "I remember you, I think."

"And I remember you, and your brothers." Fiona looked up. Mordred stood tall and shadowed in the hall, his arms crossed, face unsmiling. He dropped his head in the littlest nod.

"Mordred, of course. And Fenris."

Behind her, Laufeia felt or heard Mordred stiffen. But Fiona only thrust a bundle wordlessly from under her cloak into Laufeia's arms. As Laufeia took it, bewildered, Fiona crossed the room to the slim figure afraid in the rear of the kitchen, and with the gentlest touch she put her arms around him.

They all remained frozen for a long while in that tableau: Fiona embracing Fenris like a sister, Laufeia and Mordred standing wonderstruck. Then Fiona stepped away and turned to Laufeia, unshed tears in her eyes. "I am sorry," she said softly, "so sorry."

It was not a plea of forgiveness or an awkward platitude. It was the purest compassion Laufeia had ever heard.

~

Fiona reached up to unfasten the clasp of her cloak. Mordred strode forward, lifting it off her shoulders as it came loose, folding it with her shawl across a shelf, and leading her into the living-room. All that time, his face was a defiant mask, and he spoke no word.

She had offered to leave, supposing she had interrupted their supper, but Laufeia protested at once. “I have barely begun to ready it,” she exclaimed. “Stay, please stay. Stay for the meal, even.” So Fiona found herself following a silent, tense young man into the little living-room and sitting down with him and Fenris, while Laufeia made preparations.

Swishing and clattering came from the kitchen, pleasant, busy sounds. Here, it was quiet.

“Fred thinks that Mordred Kenhelm is suffering . . . ”

Aye, he was. Fiona watched his locked features, the eyes that slid obstinately away from her own. Where was the humorous young man who had teased Braegon the night of the wedding? Could she bring that back? She did not know. She could not take him in her arms like a babe, the way it had come so easy with Fenris, nor tear down his wall when he was not ready to relinquish it himself.

So she folded her hands lightly in her lap and spoke of little things instead. Marcus’ teasing, the house-cleaning with Peony, her four-year-old encounter with a high-strung horse.

“You lived on a farm?” Mordred shut his mouth sharply on the words, as though he had not meant to speak them and would have liked to take them back.

“Our family’s manor,” she answered with a shake of the head. “My father ruled a small tract.”

Curiosity spurted in Mordred’s eyes again. “A manor, a title—and you left all that?”

Again, she shook her head. “It is not ours any longer. That has all gone into the past.”

"It has all gone into the past, little Fianhge." Bardrick's hand stroking her shoulder, Bardrick's voice firm. "It was gone since you were a mere seven-ling. You are not a lady of Erahar anymore . . . "

Laufeia entered with a vibrant step. "The stew will cook on its own now," she said. "You are well, Fiona Segelas? And what of your family?"

Her eager, earnest chatter suddenly filled the little room with life. Under the frank disclosure of a myriad little things and trivial matters, Fiona realized how deeply Laufeia had been needing to talk to another woman. The tug of regret she felt surrendering her efforts to reach Mordred, just when his guard had been faltering, dwindled to naught. Sorrow and joy swelled her heart to bursting. *How glad I am that I came*!

"Laufeia," she said as dinner ended and she rose to leave, embracing the other girl, "I shall come again soon."

"You have done more than you know, Fiona." Laufeia's eyes were brimming with tears and gratitude.

But it was Mordred who saw her to the door. There in the dimness he spoke, low, fierce, desperate.

"How did you do that?" he said. "How did you make Fenris happy—happier than he has been since—when I have done nothing to help him—And I, I would have badgered you all your time here, would have thrown you out of the house—"

His voice broke away. He stooped in a swift, impassioned movement and kissed her on the brow, only to spring back, hurried, shaken. "Forgive me—"

"No." She touched his shoulder, soothing him with her words as she would have a child. "'Twas nothing amiss. I understand."

“I was only—so grateful.”

“Hush, aye, hush. I know.”

“Forgive me.” His voice broke again, his eyes meaning the first wrong, the deeper wrong.

“I forgive you. ’Tis all right. I understand.”

CHAPTER SIX

"I DON' KNOW IF I want you to marry her." Jerithan propped his chin on his hands and stared across the table at his brother.

"You like her, don't you?" Kenneth stared back into Jerithan's resentful hazel eyes, wondering how two people could be born of the same parents, yet be so different. Dark hair and blond hair, brown eyes and hazel eyes, slim build and—even at six years old it was plain—stocky build. A comfortable, structured, rule-bound approach to life; a restless mind filled with spurts of energy, never satisfied with knowing less than all.

"Course I like her," Jerithan muttered. "I guess."

Kenneth heaved a sigh and turned his attention to his breakfast.

"I just don' want to live with her," said Jerithan bluntly.

Exasperation needled Kenneth again, pushing toward the surface. Did Jerithan expect him to break off the betrothal?

Marianne would tell him to be patient. "What about living with her wouldn't you like?"Jerithan shrugged. "I would have two people telling me what to do."

"We wouldn't be telling you new things to do," said Kenneth. "We'd just—"

"Tell them to me double," said Jerithan.

Kenneth stood, barely containing his frustration under a stormily quiet front. "I need to leave. If Marianne comes by, maybe she can talk to you about learning to accept parts of your life that aren't how you want them to be."

"You're mad at me," said Jerithan.

Kenneth's anger melted at the small tone. "I'm sorry," he answered and bent down to give his little brother a quick hug. "Good-bye."

"Good-bye, Kenneth," replied Jerithan, waving as Kenneth opened the door.

~

Mordred had been alone by the window for half an hour or more. The old wooden shutters were flung wide as Laufeia approached him, letting dawn light into the dim room. His eyes were wide and unseeing, his mouth a thin clenched line.

"Mordred," she said gently.

No reply.

"Mordred," repeated Laufeia. "The food is waiting. Are you going to eat before you go?"

He was silent until she was sure he would refuse. At last he turned, brushing past her, and moved towards the kitchen.

She caught at his sleeve. "Mordred, I cannot bear this much longer. You must stop letting it torture you so."

"No?" He jerked away. "Is there one reason why it should not torture me? I cannot give him comfort, Laufeia, I, who would have given my life for him, can give him nothing!"

"To see you grieve like this only upsets him worse, Mordred. You, of all people, should know that."

Again, she touched him, and again he pulled away. "I do know it," he said passionately. "And I suppose you think that you can lift from me this torment? Would that you could, would that anyone could—"

She broke in desperately on his words as they spilled over one another, threatening to grow incoherent. "Mordred, come, eat, or you will be late for work."

At the close of a silent breakfast, as Mordred turned to the door, Fenris got up. "Mordred," he said.

Mordred stalled at once, his hand on the door-handle, waiting.

"Mordred," Fenris said again, "let me come with you."

Mordred stared at him.

Laufeia was no less astonished than he. Fenris' strength was gaining steadily enough, but two days ago he could scarcely lift his head in one stranger's presence. How did he think to face a whole assembly of eyes?

"Not yet, Fenris, surely," Mordred said. "Are you ready?"

"I think—" Fenris hesitated. "I think I am strong enough, Mordred."

"Not just strength, Fenris."

Fenris' eyes had always been a mirror to his heart. In their somber, smoke-grey depths lay a shrinking fear and a desperate resolve. "I must go someday, Mordred. If I can bear the first time, it will not be so bad the others."

Laufeia watched Mordred's anxious gaze probe deeply into Fenris', watched him yield with a sigh.

"All right, Fenris. If you grow tired, if you must stop early, tell me."

"Yes, Mordred."

So the two of them walked out into the clouded February morning.

~

Therelane Grey came often to the castle grounds. He would sit or stand aimlessly by the wall, listening to the men talk, waiting for one to ask him for assistance. Of course, they never did.

When the reinstatement and the castle repair of Ceristen took place, no one expected the Grey family to assist the efforts, nor did they move to do so. They were rich descendants of the old lord of Ceristen, and had no need to labor for their bread; and if their wealth were not enough, half were afflicted with the curse, rendering some unable to work and others wholly disinclined. Yet ever since the rebuilding had begun, Therelane had come day after day to watch, hoping that something would happen to break down the wall, to make him one of them.

How he wanted to be one of them.

"Gallert!" Braegon called to Lucas Boccin's son. "There's a need for the plumb line by the postern gate."

"I'll be but a moment," Gallert responded lazily, dusting his hands on his knees.

"Cease your dawdling, Gallert," said Bardrick in good-humored scolding, "before they freeze to death atop that arch."

Gallert huffed and strode away to deliver the cord to Braegon's waiting hands.

Therelane watched in envy.

He envied their companionship: he had never had one to call his friend. He envied their openness and freedom: they were all accepted, they were welcome among one another, and he? He was a prisoner in his house and an outcast when he left it. He envied even their trials. Since his birth, he had never experienced want or loss. The hard knocks of life that had taught them how to survive had never come his way. What if he were one day bereft of his place? What would happen when he tried to fend on his own?

"I cannot take care of myself," he whispered, looking at the cold courtyard stones. "I want to, but I am afraid to have to learn."

If only his father had been an Earle, a Stafford, or even a nobody from Harotha. Anything but a Grey.

The gate squeaked, shutting off his morose pools of thought, and Mordred Kenhelm's tall, haughty-faced person entered the courtyard, followed by a second figure. Therelane's interest stirred. So the oft-mentioned brother had finally recovered! He edged sideways, curious to see better. Would the two Kenhelms be much alike?

But Fenris Kenhelm was a spindly, disappointing sight. Even his resemblance to Mordred, clear as it was, only made him look timider next to his brother's forthright presence. As man after man of the work force clustered curiously around them, his pallid cheeks flushed, his eyes dropped, and a nervous shiver racked his frame.

Spineless.

Heavy footsteps stormed across the courtyard, and Therelane's glance skipped to the foreman. Maybe, he amended with a touch of pity, the boy's agitation was not wholly unfounded.

"Kenhelm! You're late."

"I apologize, sir." There was no apology in Mordred's tone.

The foreman's blunt features darkened angrily. "You think work is a pretty picnic? Here if you want, gone if you don't, eh? Thought you were entitled to some rest because I kicked you off early last night?"

Mordred's chin tilted higher, the usual sarcasm in his tone oddly constrained and replaced with acute stiffness. "Sir, if you did not notice, my brother has accompanied me today; I set the pace easy for his sake. Surely you would prefer two laborers, a mere handful of minutes late, above one faultlessly punctual?"

"Two laborers, indeed!" the foreman snorted, casting a caustic eye over Fenris. "What's he going to do, dust the courtyard? I've seen fleas with more brawn. Send your scar-faced brat back to his wet-nurse, Kenhelm, and bring him along when he's ready to do a man's work."

Fenris cowered back from the loud, blustering words, his hand rising unsteadily to cover the disfigurement or forestall a blow. But the hideous silence that thundered down over the watching men had nothing to do with Fenris.

Mordred was as still as a frozen statue: not a calm stillness, but a savage, seething stillness about to splinter into irreparable shards. He clenched his hands until the tendons stood out like cords, his thin lips ashen, his nostrils dilated. His rage swept across the courtyard in a tight, stifling current, like the smothered quiet before a squall, and every moment seemed like it must be the breaking point—but the silence only built higher, and Mordred did not stir.

The foreman alone seemed undismayed by the storm of anger directed at him. He waited with threateningly folded arms for the coming, unforgivable insubordination.

"Mordred!" The call, snapping so clear and carefree across the rigid atmosphere, jolted them all. It was Braegon King who came from behind the keep.

In an instant, his quick dark eyes had apprised the scene. "Mordred?" he repeated with a quiet firmness.

The anger ebbed out of Mordred's face, leaving it empty, almost unconscious. He pivoted with the slowness of a man half-asleep and took a step towards Braegon.

"I need a hand getting this rubble in the cart," explained Braegon with a gesture behind the keep. He waited for Mordred's nod, and turned to lead the way. They disappeared from view.

Like a slackened bowstring, the strain in the air dissipated. The leaden day seemed bright and welcoming; the men turned back to their own tasks, and a pleasant hum of activity resurged. The foreman, evidently feeling that matters had fared to his success, departed with satisfied stance to oversee the wall construction.

Therelane, too, released a long breath, his shoulders easing. And then a flash of apprehension jolted him, and his gaze whipped back to the solitary figure forgotten by the gate.

What about Fenris?

The boy stood staring after Mordred, shoulders squared with a forlorn bravery that lasted for a few valiant moments, and then caved. He turned quickly, head bowed, and hid his face against the wall. Therelane's heart panged for him; he was glad to see Mr. Earle leave off talking with Edrach Stafford and approach the sorry figure with a gentle touch.

Fenris whirled like a spooked colt. But Mr. Earle only beckoned him to follow, leading him across the stones, past the work crew, up to, up to—

"Me!" exclaimed Therelane inaudibly.

"Here, Therelane," said Mr. Earle. "He can stay with you for the present. Edrach and I are off to have words with the foreman; we'll see afterwards what the lad can do." With that, he left.

Therelane stared at Fenris, knowing he should be glad to have someone give him a task, wishing it had been any other task. He reached out to take his arm in an awkward attempt at companionship, but Fenris flinched and Therelane pulled hastily back.

"Would you . . ." His voice trailed. "There is a little niche over that way, behind the castle," he said finally. "We could get away from all these eyes."

No answer came for a long, unpleasant stretch; the color began to build in Therelane's face. At last Fenris dropped his head in the barest nod.

The recess, formed by the base of two high towers at the back of the keep, was quiet and sheltered from the wind. Therelane sat against one of the towering buttresses of dark rock, and, hesitantly, Fenris followed his example. Therelane relaxed; perhaps they could make headway after all. He tried again, placing a cautious hand on Fenris' arm. Again, Fenris started, but after the initial movement he was still and let the hand remain there, though Therelane felt him trembling.

What is the matter with him? Therelane pulled away, perturbed with both Fenris and himself.

"My name is Therelane Grey," he said.

Fenris nodded.

"And you are Fenris Kenhelm?"

Again, the dark head twitched in acknowledgment.

A thought occurred to him, and he felt compelled to voice it—as kindly as he could. "Can you talk?"

Fenris' eyes, dark and cheerless as rainclouds, dropped with a small shiver. "Aye."

All the things Therelane thought of saying after that would only have made the moment worse. So he said nothing. A heavy, blanketing, almost drowsy silence unrolled between them.

Therelane's tension evaporated under the peaceful totality of the stillness. With the outer world far away and the wind whispering somewhere above the towers, he forgot to be embarrassed, forgot his annoyance; he all but forgot that Fenris was there. He was not sure when he started talking, only knew distantly that he had been at it for a while: rambling, voicing the things he said to himself, the woods, and the horse.

" . . . Of course, I love Lewis and Adolphus. They are not mad, after all, nor even curse-touched, and they are my brothers. And it seems as though all that ought to bring us together. But with six years between us, it is no use. They do not need me; they have one another's company, and care nothing for mine . . .

"As for Irene, she may not be mad, but she is so brusque, so endlessly impatient. Her harm-sensing gift sours her into the mood of a jaded old crone who has time for nothing but practicalities. She calls me a wasteful dreamer—and maybe I am. But if she would only stop and listen!"

"I am sorry you are lonely," said Fenris, startling Therelane out of his half-conscious tirade— "I have never been lonely. Mordred was always there."

An unexpected life came over his face as he pronounced his brother's name. The melancholy eyes awoke, the thin features lifted; even his soft tone lost its shyness and deepened with burning love. He looked as though he would smile, and Therelane felt himself waiting expectantly, almost anxiously, for that smile.

But the moment sped like a flash of sun on a dark day, and Fenris' countenance seemed more pathetic than ever after its fleeting transfiguration, the bones sharper, the eyes more unhappy. The scar, a grotesque ridge dark with scabs and pocked with stitching, glared out in a way Therelane had not noticed before.

He could not help himself: it was so prominent, so stark and repulsive in its nearness. He stared.

Fenris stared back, the quiet puzzlement in his eyes shattering to comprehension and terror. His hand flew up, palm outward like a shield, and a nervous spasm convulsed his frame. He buried his head on his knees, body taut and shaking.

Therelane's indignation slowly simmered. While a part of him felt that he had been wrong to look, had it really warranted such a reaction? He had not made fun of him. Why, this whole time he had scarcely glanced at the scar, and it was not his fault he had suddenly noticed it! Fenris must be seventeen—sixteen at the least—what kind of grown lad threw a tantrum at a little look?

He swallowed back the frustration, waiting until the shuddering had subsided, and laid a hand gingerly on Fenris' shoulder. Fenris flung himself back and huddled against the stones.

The indignation came sweeping straight back, scorching a trail of disgust through Therelane's innards. So now Fenris wanted to sit and sulk! Well, let him; let him hate Therelane for one accidental glance; let him nurse his feelings in morbid seclusion. Why, why was he such a baby?

He sucked in a deep, audible breath and began to talk desultorily of anything that came to mind, hoping that Fenris would sit up and act in a sensible fashion. When the welcome footsteps came behind him, he glanced up, relieved that Mr. Earle or Edrach Stafford had come at last.

But it was neither Earle nor Stafford who stood behind him.

Mordred's eyes burned hotly in a face white and set as they fell on Therelane, who rose to his feet and took a step back, remembering the anger of earlier.

"I was—I was talking to him," he said lamely. "Keeping him company a little."

"I see," replied Mordred in a voice cold enough to crack stone.

"Mr. Earle told me to," stammered Therelane, though he knew Mordred Kenhelm was the last person to be appeased by his blame-shifting.

"I see," said Mordred scornfully. He strode past to Fenris and put an arm around his shoulders. Fenris, who had stood as soon as he heard his brother's voice, looked up at him with those dreary eyes.

Mordred spoke to him awhile in tones too low to carry, leaving Therelane to wonder in sickening dread what was passing between them, until at last Braegon arrived unnoticed and departed shortly with Fenris. Then Mordred turned back to Therelane.

"Therelane Grey," he stated, with less fury, though his voice was still cold and dangerous. "You spoke with my brother."

"Aye," answered Therelane nervously.

"So. What do you think of him? What everyone else thinks? What a shame? What a shame that he is so weak? Frightened? Spineless?" Therelane flinched as he heard the description of his own devising delivered with such scathing ferocity. "Stupid? Slow? Skittish?"

Mordred halted only for a breath. "Why can't he speak when spoken to? Why does he let himself sink into dejection rather than stand up and take his sufferings like a man?"

He cut off Therelane's attempt. "No. I don't want to hear your excuses. I don't want your empty denials of everything you don't think. Tell me what you *do* think of my brother."

Therelane drew in an unsteady breath. "If you want my honest opinion, you shall have it. I—I am sorry for Fenris. I would not want to be in his place. As for shyness, well, if anyone can understand shyness it is I. But—" He hesitated, looking at those pale, taut features.

He asked me. "But he takes it so far. The lightest touch might as well be a branding iron, and one wrong look sends him into a fit of panic.

A boy his age ought to have more backbone than that. Why does he act as if I mean him harm? He's a—" He could not bring himself to say coward to Mordred's dreadful face. "As timid as a rabbit kit. It almost looks as if he's seeking to curry pity. But," he added hastily, "since you're his brother, you would know better than I do."

The muscles in Mordred's jaw worked silently in and out.

"So that is what you think, is it?" he said at last. "What would you think if your whole life long no one had lifted a hand except to slap you? If all your seventeen years you had been taunted and harassed by children because you were small and vulnerable, and beaten and reviled by adults because they had demanded from you the work of someone your size and half again? If in all those seventeen years there were only two people who loved you, one of whom you hardly ever saw? And the one you did see"—Mordred's throat caught like a snapping twig—"could never help you?"

I didn't know, Therelane wanted to say, but he could not speak.

When Mordred began again, he sounded gentler and more tired than Therelane had ever heard him. "We lived in Rehirne," he said. "Our parents came from elsewhere, but we children were birthed and raised in Rehirne. And for a time, it was not so bad in Rehirne, even if we were poor; the rest of that village after all was little better off. They, our parents, were young, empty-headed things who neither cared for us nor cared to work, so we learned to fend for ourselves and knew nothing better. And then we were orphaned."

Mordred looked sharply at Therelane. "I suppose you know nothing of Rehirne."

He did not wait for an answer. "Orphans are shunned. They are unclean, despised, a defilement on the earth. Why? Because it is convenient. All the ills of society can be blamed on an orphan. They used to fill the streets, until some lauded person took notice and suggested that they pay for their crime against society by work. So now they lock the orphans away and give them the work no one else will do. Perhaps they are fed one day, perhaps not another day, since after all, what does an orphan deserve? If they cannot work, they are beaten. If they die, who cares? It was only another orphan.

"My brother—my little brother, so sensitive, so full of gentleness—they put out all the light in his eyes. They crushed him."

He was quiet for so long, Therelane thought at first he was finished.

"Months ago, we escaped. We fled our orphanage, we fled Rehirne, we came here. And Fenris was brightening, he was daring to lift up his head—and now this—"

He did not think Mordred knew he was there anymore. The young man's lips moved in the silence, forming almost inaudible words. *"Would that it had been me . . . "*

And Therelane, who had begun to understand so much in the past fleeting minutes, understood that Mordred was in need of far deeper help than Fenris. His heart reached out, shivering and urgent, as if it had been his own brother that stood there. "Mordred," he breathed, stretching out a hand.

The stillness cracked, and the foreman's angry shout rolled around him. "Kenhelm! At it again, are you? Get out here this minute and get to work!"

Therelane's heart leaped halfway to his mouth in startlement, and in dread of Mordred's biting reply. But Mordred only turned with a quiet "Aye, sir."

The proud shoulders were drooping as he walked.

~

Therelane's mind was alive, burning with Mordred's words. His own blindness and Mordred's answer revisited him moment by moment with strange, wondering clarity. He scarcely knew when he left the castle and trudged towards home. The castle, the road, even himself, none of them seemed to matter. Not against the reflections in his head.

And then, tumbling from the whirl of vivid introspection, one thing flashed out and halted him in his tracks. The one thing Fenris had said to him.

"I'm sorry that you are lonely."

Why, Fenris had been listening to his whole self-centered tirade!

The more Therelane thought about it, the more incredible it seemed. Fenris had listened, had cared, had responded with sympathy. Sympathy for Therelane? For a life of pleasure, kindness, and ease that he had never known?

Therelane was shamed . . . and glad.

Glad for Fenris' sake.

CHAPTER SEVEN

THE BOARDED WINDOW RATTLED IN the night wind. Overhead, the ceiling creaked; Ledelia must be pacing her room.

Therelane lay restless under two stifling comforters, hearing Mordred with every beat of his thundering heart. With evening, the spiral of his thoughts had turned inward, instead of the strange outward bent they had had all afternoon. While before he had been absorbed utterly on the Kenhelms and how he had done by them, now he started to worry. He started to ponder what they must think of him.

What were Mordred Kenhelm's feelings tonight? What kind of hate was he harboring towards the blind, idiotic young man who had hurt him, provoked him to desperation, and witnessed every second of his shattering humiliation?

Therelane rolled over, burying his face against the hot pillow in wretched frustration. Mordred had no idea that Therelane's mind had changed, and the thought of trying to explain to him, the thought of even approaching that dreadful, anger-pale face, provoked a cold sweat and a knot of denial in his innards. If he had only realized what he was doing when he said all those callous, condemnatory words about Fenris! Had he been mad? As good as mad, to slander a man's brother to his face when the man looked like he was ready to kill at any moment!

Even if he did force himself to explain, what good would it do? Therelane could hear his own fumbling efforts, could see Mordred's cool, entirely disbelieving eyebrows arched in denial. No, Mordred would not think him sorry for a moment.

But that word—sorry—seemed to pierce the tangle with a whole new element. Indeed, it severed the tangle quite simply and threw it away, and Therelane found himself standing in the still black lucidity outside the circle of self.

If he were sorry, he needed to apologize.

No matter what Mordred, Fenris, or anyone else thought of him. Therelane had erred; he would have to make amends.

~

The sun rose molten in the dawn, cold over the frozen earth. A warm day had ended in a frigid night, and little droplets of ice were frozen on the edge of every fir needle and every bare twig. As Therelane walked slowly to the castle, soft frost-borne breezes rubbed them against one another, and they tingled faintly.

As early as Therelane had set out, the Kenhelms were already there when he came through the gate. He started forward, and checked, staring at Mordred.

Mordred's eyes, always so alert and cold, were dull. His shoulders hung. To the foreman, who snapped out his instructions with a baleful eye, he responded only with an apathetic nod. What had happened to his walls of impassivity and scorn? For they were walls—they had come down yesterday. Therelane had seen it. He had seen the fury come lashing out until it burned itself away into grief-stricken embers.

Like now.

Except that then, Mordred had been tense. Fighting back the pain. Now there was no fight in his eyes, only misery. All the bitterness that had come rushing out yesterday, locked away for so long, had left him spent, and he had nothing left. No one to give him relief; no one to turn to, no friends.

This was of my making. The thought filled Therelane with alarm, verging on horror. The need to make reparation, to mend his wrongs, burned in him with guilty urgency.

He hurried forward as the older Kenhelm made for the back of the keep, catching him alone at the corner. "Mordred!"

Mordred whipped around, his features hardening into a semblance of their old mask. When he saw Therelane, his eyes narrowed. "Aye?" The flat, contemptuous tone goaded him to speak. *Go on,* it said. *Humiliate me some more.*

The outright mockery took Therelane aback. All the fears of last night, half-forgotten and dismissed, swarmed up again, and his resolve buckled.

Why go on? He could already hear the sarcasm-laden reply. Mordred did not want an apology; Mordred had already said he did not want "excuses and denials." All Mordred cared about was making every other person as unhappy as himself.

Then Therelane remembered the gentleness in the young man's tired voice the day before, and all the clamoring inner voices fell strangely silent.

"My words yesterday were spoken in discourtesy and unpardonable ignorance, Mordred Kenhelm," he said. "For them I beg your pardon."

Mordred looked away. "You have it," he said without interest.

Therelane lunged forward and seized his arm. "Mordred, wait!"

Mordred shrugged stiffly free, still not looking at him. "Aye. What more do you want?"

"Mordred, I—I was very wrong in what I thought of Fenris. I disregarded his suffering, no—worse than that, I despised it for weakness. I was thinking only of myself. I hurt him when he needed kindness and comfort; he offered me comfort, and I turned my back on it. I was blind to his struggles, to your struggles, and to his compassion." Hearing the faults spoken from his own mouth branded them anew on his heart, and his throat tightened in grief for the pain that he had thoughtlessly inflicted. All at once, it seemed the most vital thing in the world to reach the distant face before him with solace.

"I thought he was a selfish weakling. I thought that he had given up. I was wrong. Mordred, your brother is not gone. He may be broken, but he is still there. It looks to you as though this scar has crushed him again, left him a shell, and there is nothing left, but it is not so. He is still fighting. He is still Fenris. He moved past his fear to reach out to me, he gave me understanding. Mordred, he is not gone." Therelane broke off, breathless and stuttering over his own words, the tightness in his throat near to tears, hardly knowing himself any longer. In a moment he started again, more steadily.

"I hurt you too, Mordred, not just with my words, but with my careless treatment of Fenris. Please, Mordred, I know you feel alone, even if I cannot understand fully. But you are not alone. There is Braegon, at least; he cares for you, he would be your friend if you let him. There is Mr. Earle, I think, and maybe others. And, Mordred, please—there is also me."

Mordred had not moved once this whole time. At Therelane's words, his head lifted in a quick, imperceptible movement, and a hint of life sprang into his clear grey eyes. "You, Therelane?" he repeated.

Therelane bit his lip and nodded.

"You have put me to shame," said Mordred simply. "What is there to say?"

"Say nothing," said Therelane. "You need say nothing at all. The fault was mine."

Mordred shook his head. "Forgive me my anger towards you, Therelane, and the resentment I entertained of you last night." He spoke with a swift, eager earnestness. "My words were said harshly and in haste."

"I do forgive you for any wrong you did," Therelane answered. "Harshly, maybe; yet but for your harshness, I might not have understood."

Mordred nodded. The life had not left his eyes. A release settled throughout his whole frame, like tension that leaves a sail when the storm is gone, yet he stood taller than before. "Therelane," he said, laying a hand on Therelane's shoulder. "Thank you."

~

"Kenhelm! Get your lazy self over here!"

Mordred looked up from his shaping, face stiffening at the address. "Aye, sir," he answered with a quiet restraint, and he laid down his chisel to join the group of three others as they strained to heave a block into place. The foreman gave him a startled eye, which he scorned to notice.

Let the foreman insult him. Let him deride him. Mordred liked him no better than before, but he was never going to give him an insolent answer again.

He liked even less the surprised glances that came his way from the other men. Did they think him beyond the capacity to be civil? He returned to his own task when the stone was laid, deliberately meeting none of their stares.

But neither dull-witted stares nor the tedium of stone-cutting could drive away the quiet, pervasive sense of peace. He braced one hand against the narrow ledge of granite, tapping steadily with the chisel, sweeping away the stray fragments; and under it was the peace, strange and whole.

Whenever his eyes fell on Therelane, the cold waves of hope that the other young man had brought crashed over him afresh, mingled with the warmer surge of gratitude. Each time he sent the watching figure a glad smile and set about his work with vigor renewed.

It struck him, in one of those brief glances, the awareness of how solitary Therelane looked; how he stood against the wall, arms loosely folded, wistful gaze wandering over the activity of the courtyard. Did he come like this every day? Why was he not counted with the work crew? What brought him here?

A memory shifted, a shadowy image from the night he and Braegon had gone to fetch help for Fenris: Irene Grey snatching a cloak from its peg in a flash of crimson, and Therelane behind her, a dim presence in the hall, eyes doubtful under the golden lamp-light. A Grey, heir of the past lord's inheritance. A sane Grey, not afflicted with the curse.

No wonder he would leave that house. Mordred remembered the dark structure and the eerie, uncontrolled laugh echoing in the night. No wonder he would quit those walls to seek companionship, when he could not find it among his own kin. Yet there he waited by the wall, unacknowledged and friendless.

A deep, unconscious instinct stirred in Mordred, and he left his chiseling and took a step toward Therelane.

"Therelane!" he called. "Will you come and help me hold this steady?"

Therelane came—his eyes bright, his face wonder-filled.

"It goes quicker with two," said Mordred easily as they worked. He looked at Therelane and a wide, teasing smile cracked over his face. Therelane broke into a foolish grin in answer

Mordred tilted back his head and laughed. "You look like a sheep," he said.

~

"Ai!" exclaimed Braegon in alarm as Fenris started and the bore slipped. He stooped quickly to retrieve it and set it to the slab again. "Fenris, are you harmed?"

"No," Fenris stammered, whirling, scanning the whole courtyard. "No—I am sorry."

Braegon watched him, perplexed. "What is it?" he gently queried.

Fenris spoke with soft intensity. "I heard Mordred laugh."

~

Laufeia bent over the warming pottage, ladle in hand; heat rose up into her face, curling the wisps of hair around it. She turned as the door grated open in signal of the boys' return.

Mordred sauntered in ahead of Fenris, shrugged the snow lazily from his coat, and flashed a wide-open grin at her.

Laufeia dropped the ladle in shock. She could not speak or even gasp.

"A fine welcome you give, sister," he said, a teasing light from older days in his eyes, though he spoke rather gently. He reached out a hand and ruffled the top of her head.

She slapped his hand away and stared at him still.

"Are you not going to greet me, Laufeia?"

"I hardly know you," she whispered.

"That is my fault. I have not been helping you on this long climb up, have I, Laufeia? Forgive me."

Her eyes filled with tears. They spilled over and ran helplessly down her cheeks, and he pulled her close, comforting.

"Te adda rine bocca murat, tu adda rine lech," he murmured against her hair. "But we will see it through together."

~

It was strangely like coming home, the wedding. People looked at her, smiled at her, even greeted her with warmth, as though the joy of the day had cast a sudden inviting spell over the world. Laufeia was bewildered and exhilarated by it. All at once she could talk to people. They could talk to her. And there was no wall between them.

"Are you glad you came?" Mirda asked her as, with the ceremony complete, the watching people broke up into chattering knots and the women began to ready the food.

"Yes," said Laufeia, an open, free smile breaking over her face. It felt wonderful to smile again. "Yes, I am, Mirda. Oh, it is good to talk to people."

Mirda's smile brightened in answer, and she put an arm around Laufeia's waist. "Did neither of your brothers come? Fenris must be easily tired yet, but I thought that Mordred might accompany you."

Laufeia bit her lip. "Nay," she answered softly, "he did not want to come. He . . . you must understand, Mirda, his life is bound in Fenris'. I hardly know how to describe it aright. From the very first, it was always Fenris that he could not bear to see hurt. Mockery, hostility, beatings, he took them with head high—but not if it were Fenris. And as hard as he tried to shield him, there was so little that he could ever truly shield him from. Then, when we came here, and Fenris, the accident . . . You see, Mirda? He spent his life failing his brother, and now there is this unspeakable failure that he can never redeem. It wounded him deeply, and though the healing has begun, it will not be quick. He still feels estranged from most of the village; only Braegon and Therelane Grey, I think, does he see as friends. He is not ready to mingle yet."

"I understand," said Mirda. "I will tell this to Braegon, if you do not mind. He has only guessed at most of it till now."

"Your brother is wise, Mirda."

Mirda gave a little bubbling laugh. "I know. I tell him so, but he thinks he has no more sense than anyone else. Though a sharp temper he may have at times, truly, Laufeia, I believe Braegon is the humblest man on the face of the earth."

"Laufeia Kenhelm, isn't it?" Mrs. Earle poked her plump form between them. "What lovely hair you have, my dear. Have I told you so before?"

"No, ma'am, I don't think so." Laufeia did not think Mrs. Earle had ever spoken to her before.

"Sometimes I forget I've told a person something," explained Mrs. Earle candidly. "And your brother, young Fenris, how is he?"

"He is doing much better, thank you." It was the first time, she realized a moment later, that she had been able to answer that question without a sense of nervous dread.

"Aye, now that's welcome news." Her soft cheeks split under a cheery smile to the time of her bobbing head. "Arad says that he is even well enough to help on the castle work now?"

Laufeia nodded. "That is true."

Mrs. Earle reached out and brushed Laufeia's cheek, unexpectedly and gently. "Well, I will say, dear, that you are a brave girl, a brave, strong girl, and there's not a woman alive who shouldn't admire you for all you're taking on." With a pat to Laufeia's shoulder, she moved away.

"I didn't even congratulate her about her daughter," murmured Laufeia, bemused.

"Oh! 'tis no matter," said Mirda. "She will certainly not remember, or if she does, she will not think any ill of you for it. Mrs. Earle is a deal more sharp-witted than she seems, for all her chatter; but she is a very kind and well-meaning woman."

"I like her," said Laufeia, meaning far more than the words said. What words could express the lightness awash within her?

"Look!" Mirda gestured out to the middle of the room as it began to clear. "There is Lucas Boccin bringing out his pipes for the dancing. I suppose Braegon will come to fetch me shortly." She laughed, in her sunny, exuberant way, and tapped her foot expectantly to the cadence of the music.

"A man and a woman did not dance together in Fearnland," she went on. "It is so different here, but I love it all the same. Look, there go Kenneth and Marianne first of anyone, and Samantha and her husband right behind. And the Segelases are not afraid to dance; I see Bardrick bringing Peony out onto the floor, and Fiona with Marcus. Why, no! Fiona is with Fred."

"Fiona!" said Laufeia, at once interested.

"Aye. You would not know her much yet?"

"A little," said Laufeia, the warm, lamplit memory welling in her mind.

"At any rate, there she is. I have never seen Fred dance before. They do look well together," Mirda remarked thoughtfully.

Laufeia raised her eyebrows. "Mirda, what are you saying?"

Mirda gave a girlish giggle. "I am given to pairing now and again. I would not be sorry to see Braegon's good friend courting the fair lady of Erahar."

The silliness, the high spirits, swept Laufeia up, and she laughed unbidden. Then she laughed again, in wonder, because she could.

~

"Do you, then, like to dance?" Fiona asked, her dark eyes questioning.

"I have never danced," he answered, fumbling in his step even as he spoke. "But this seemed a slow one, and I thought that I would give you the pleasure, my lady Fiona."

Fiona's radiant, unconscious smile stole over her face, transforming its repose into a living beauty, and a soft flush came transparently to her cheek. "I thank you for that, Fred Thorne."

He smiled in answer. "Your appreciation for such a small gift is even more beautiful, my lady."

"More beautiful than what?" Her delicate bird's-wing brows drew together, and suddenly the color came rushing into her face in a confused blush, and she lowered her eyes. "Again—I thank you," she stammered.

"You are welcome, my lady Fiona." He sought to alleviate her embarrassment with the words. Yet there was something gently appealing and lovely even in her shyness. "Truly, I have never met a maid as fair as you, Fiona, nor one whose company I have enjoyed more."

He stared at her, somewhat astonished himself at what he had said. But he had meant it.

They stood, looking speechlessly at one another, blushing hotly. Then the tension broke, and Fiona buried her face in her hands with a spurt of nervous laughter.

How foolish they must have looked. Fred found a rueful chuckle escaping him as he took her arm and attempted to find their place in the dance.

CHAPTER EIGHT

THE SUN OF HIGH NOON beat down on the whitened road and on a tall, lean figure who wandered aimlessly down its windings.

"I shall not be gone too long, Fenris."

Of course not.

"I might go see whether there is any work to do for hire, if not everyone has gone to the wedding."

He might.

"It is all right if you only want to walk alone, Mordred."

"I might do that."

He might.

Other memories seeped around that of his conversation with Fenris, weaving in and out in quick, elusive fragments, worming their way to the forefront. They had been stirring at the edges of his mind for several days now, even as he steadfastly avoided acknowledging them, not wanting the excitement to return before he had a chance to act. Now, alone on the road, they flooded back to him in full—the rabbit at the noon break a se'ennight past, the dark, forbidding house, the strange secret aura about it, the carvings on the walls.

He wheeled around and strode up the path, step swift and sure.

The black, spired peak jutted up like a menacing claw-finger into the grey sky when he edged out of the trees, tiny flakes of snow whirling around it and drifting down. It looked the same as before, just as dark, just as silent.

Yet Mordred walked up to the door, hesitated before it with his breath coming hard and rapid, and knocked.

For a long time there was no answer; he almost turned away. Then all at once it flew open, and she stood there, barring his way, a tall and proud-faced woman of angular build, with rough, tawny hair falling heavy and unbound over her shoulders. Her face was not beautiful, but it riveted his gaze in the unexpected eagerness that pulsed throughout it.

"Aye?" Her voice was clear and cold and humming with a faint expectancy. "What?"

The words took him aback. It was as though she expected him to be someone else. "I am Mordred Kenhelm, my lady," he said slowly. "Have you any work for me to do?"

She drew back, looking at him with changed expression. Her narrow eyes bored into his, alarm or anger flashing through them, and her hand clenched around the handle.

He took a quick step forward, his curiosity rushing higher still. "Will you at least call your husband?"

"I have neither son nor husband," she said. "Begone!"

"If you will—" he persisted.

"Begone!" she cried harshly and slammed the door.

He stared at it a moment, at its ancient grain and dark engravings, and at last turned unwillingly and went back to the road. A deep mark of thought formed between his brows.

~

"Did you have a good time while I was gone, Mordred?"

"Oh yes." Mordred gazed at his plate.

"Fenris said you thought you might look for work; did you find any?"

"Hm? Oh. Yes."

Laufeia set her spoon down and stared directly at her brother. "Mordred when I asked you that same question two minutes ago, you said no."

Mordred murmured some unintelligible, vaguely conciliatory affirmative, and continued to study his plate. "Must not have known what I was saying."

"You don't know what you're saying now!" she retorted, near the end of her patience.

He blinked up at her, ruffled. "Yes, I do!"

"I'd like to hear you repeat it to me." Laufeia folded her arms as the silence trailed out.

Mordred broke their blank, stubborn stare first and flung up his hands. "Whatever I said, it evidently wasn't important enough to remember. Suppose we go back to eating?"

"Mordred," she said swiftly, before he could fall back into his oblivion, "what is bothering you?"

He pushed his chair back, startled and clearly vexed. "Nothing."

"I know you too well for that."

"Nothing," said Mordred distinctly, "is bothering me. I am thinking about something. That is all." *And that,* said his look, *is the end of the conversation.*

But he scarcely touched his food all evening. Time and again she watched his gaze wander straight through her, fixed on things only he could see. His eyes were bright, his nostrils flared, like a wild colt tossing his head to catch the scent of danger.

~

A windy, sun-struck morning rose over Mount Thiranu.

"Are you sure this was a wise idea?" Daren looked doubtfully around the tiny kitchen of the cottage, its dusty corners illuminated by the rays of light streaming through the open door. "Six of us already strain the limits of our table, and you want to add four more."

"Tch-tch, Daren," said Isabelle and shooed him away. "Leave the planning to the women."

"I expect to see room for our guests this evening," Daren rejoined.

"Nay, Daren; they will doubtless have transformed the place into a castle by our arrival," Fred assured him with his slight smile as they left the house.

When they returned again, late in the black evening with soft shadows and silvered clouds around the moon, Bardrick and Marcus Segelas accompanied them.

"What a night," said Marcus, breathing in the delicate winter-night tang. "I think I will stay out here instead of coming to your house."

"You have my blessing to freeze to death," said Bardrick dryly.

Fred laughed, whereupon Marcus assumed the look of a complacent cat. "Some people," he said to Bardrick, "can appreciate my humor, you see."

Bardrick turned his eyes up to the star-flecked sky and said nothing.

The Segelas girls had arrived already. When Fred and the others entered, Peony was settled comfortably with Isabelle and Sandy beside the fire, and they were all talking brightly with laughter singing over their chatter. Cecelia sat nearby them, listening with her quiet half-smile on her lips and her hands clasped around her knees. But Fiona was in the corner, veiled in its dusk, and as a stray tongue of fire flung itself out it touched on her. And Fred saw to his surprise that she was with Gwenda, and the look of earnest interest on her features caught at his heart.

What was it about each expression flitting over her face that spoke so matchlessly fair? They all seemed filled with a concentrated yet unconscious sincerity. Yes, there was a transparency in them, a wholeness and a pureness, as though her thoughts came with a truth that others' did not.

Like Cecelia, he had thought when he first met her, like Cecelia in her artlessness; but Cecelia's face was immobile, locked in a stillness that never showed emotion except what she let. Fiona's vibrated with a melody unceasing.

A quick, sharp tug came to his heart, as of beauty that one could not endure—he called to mind the distant mountains he had seen on the way to Orden, beauty like peril. Nay, there was no peril in that glowing, love-filled face. And yet it hurt in the same sharp, deep way.

He looked away, that he might not have to see the moment broken.

~

"So, what is it that you like to do when you have no work to keep you occupied?" Fiona asked the small, quiet face curiously. "How do you amuse yourself, since everyone around you is so much older?"

"They are not so much older than me," answered Gwenda, looking a little surprised. "Cecelia is fifteen years old, only four more than I am. But I like to talk to Fred, when he is here—to all of them, really. But I liked to talk to Fred and Marjorie most; now Marjorie is married, and Fred is not often here." She paused, the sweet, pointed face pensive, and then continued on eagerly, "But Marjorie began to teach me to knit with wool, like this"—she produced the beginnings of a shawl from the deep pocket in her kirtle—"and Isabelle has been teaching me more since. So I like to do that often."

"Gwenda!" Isabelle called over the bustle in the middle of the room.

And "Fiona! I do believe we're supposed to start eating . . . " came Marcus' cheerful cry.

"I thought for certain we'd have to pry you out of there with a hook and line, sister," he observed with dancing eyes as they came to the table.

A little embarrassment heated Fiona's cheeks, but she did not mind much in that moment. And Marcus touched her hand lightly with a look of hopeful apology as he sat beside her, at which she brightened with a reassuring smile.

"Well met, my lady Fiona," said Fred; and she started, for she had not noticed him sit on her other hand.

"Aye," she murmured, daring to glance at him and smile.

"So," he said as they began to eat, "you were talking to Gwenda, I saw. Did you enjoy her company?"

Fiona's face lit with the memory. "Fred, I never saw such a wonderful little girl! She is so full of innocence, yet so solemn and steady-minded. She speaks to me with respect, but almost as an equal; there is something so childish in her speech, but she speaks of things that most children would never find of interest! And when she laughs, it is in the strangest, sweetest way, as though she had never known how to laugh and had only just discovered."

Fred did not speak for a moment, but his eyes shone with emotion. After a little he said, "Would you guess, my lady Fiona, that three months ago she did not know what a name meant?"

Fiona watched him, wondering and moved. "I could almost have guessed it," she said at last. "But how was it so?"

"She is my sister, yet she lived long apart from us. She was taken by slave traders when she was but a babe, and by a strange and wonderful circumstance we found her again as we traveled through the wilderness. To look at her, it is always for me like seeing one brought back from the dead." The tears glittered in his eyes again as he spoke, and he looked across to Gwenda.

The silence trembled between them, a well of deep gladness. Fiona broke it at last, saying softly, "What was it like, this journey of yours? For it seems that your family was full of many separations, and this journey was a mending of them."

Another moment of silence passed, and Fred answered slowly, "Yes; that is a good way to say it. We are a fragmented family, pieced together again by the trip that brought us across Legea. But indeed, those were not the only cracks. There were others, and some of them will never heal."

And Fiona lowered her eyes, for he was looking on faraway things, and she did not want to betray him by watching.

"So!" said Marcus in her ear, startling her; she had quite forgotten that he was there. "How many of you were there at the beginning, that is, how many started out from your home village?"

"In Harotha," Fred responded, "we were only three: my married sister Marjorie, myself, and Sandy."

"And you grew to this?" Marcus glanced astonished around the table. "A feat indeed, my friend."

A surprisingly broad smile lightened Fred's face. "And I thank you for saying so."

"Go on, Fred," said Isabelle. "Tell them the whole story from the beginning. For I did promise it to Peony and Fiona, after all, when they called."

Fred laughed a little, seeming embarrassed at being so picked upon. Then he hesitated, and his gaze traveled across the table. "Let Sandy tell it," he said.

~

"A good time," said Marcus as they walked home under the foggy moon.

"And a good family," said Peony.

"Hm," Bardrick murmured in assent.

"Have you nothing to say, Fiona?" Marcus teased when she was silent. "What do you think of the Thornes?"

"I am glad to know them," answered Fiona slowly, almost dreamily, for her mind was deep within the memories of the things behind them. "I should be grieved if I were parted from them."

"And Fred?" said Marcus.

Fiona did not heed his intonation; her thoughts were too distant. "When I speak with Fred," she answered, "I feel as if I have never left Erahar. Nay—rather as if I could never need Erahar again."

Marcus was silent. "I'm glad for you, Fiona," he said at last, softly, and there was no teasing in his voice this time.

~

"Whose is the black house east of the castle?" Mordred said to Braegon as they sat against the wall for a breather.

Braegon looked at him, puzzled. "The black house?"

Mr. Earle answered from nearby. "You must have seen the old dwelling that the Greys built. Older than any other house on this mountain, though perhaps not so old as the castle itself; a strain of the Grey house lived there for many generations. It is abandoned now."

"Ah! I remember it now," agreed Braegon. "And indeed, I cannot think who would want to live there. 'Tis so brooding a place."

He said nothing. Nothing about the rabbit and the little crooking trail, nothing about the woman at the door who had thought he was someone else. But when the break came at noon, he told Fenris to eat without him and strode away to the gate, hurrying down the road.

This time he did not follow the little side path, but skirted the house, keeping to the trees, and approached it from the back. The sharp excitement of danger and his own recklessness quickened his senses; he was keenly aware of each movement he made, and of the consequences it might bring upon him.

He leaned under the eaves against the concealment of the black wall, searching for another way in. There, a door, away in a recess to his left. He crossed over in a few quick steps, brushed the cobwebs from the handle, and pushed it open.

A dark hall met his eyes, musty and filled with the grime of years. Cobwebs like those on the door stretched palely overhead, a few dead strands hanging across his path. All light left when he closed the door behind him, save for one sickly ray that sifted down from a high window on the far wall.

He felt his way gradually, glimpses of the house greeting him as he passed along: carven doors, murky rooms, cracked chests and crumbling tapestries, and other corridors, countless corridors, lightless halls and passageways that beckoned to him with questions of what they held.

He could not follow them all.

At one room he stopped. It had a less decayed sense than the others; torches hung burning on the walls. It was high and vaulted, and scrolls were scattered all over the floor like withered leaves, rustling at the breath of the opened door. Other things lay among them, small baubles, here and there: an ornamented dagger, a signet ring with a mark too crude to be distinguished, a cracked clay tablet. Mordred's eyes tarried on a stone slab relief— a finely embossed article full of absorbing detail. It depicted a man before a well, pillars rising up on either side of him and branches bearing all kinds of leaf and fruit arching overhead. He held a drinking vessel to his lips; four more figures stood behind him, and a blurry mark that might have been a fifth at the very edge of the carving. Mordred would have liked to go closer, to touch the weathered surface and study the intricacies that he could only guess at from here.

And yet he did not enter. Something constrained him, quelling his urge to go forward, though it did not quell his curiosity. These were her things, not his. They were her secrets to hoard, not his to uncover. For all his captivation with this house, with this woman, he knew that it was not his leave to meddle any further.

With a last look at the secret-laden room, he turned and walked away.

CHAPTER nine

THE MORNING AIR WAS STILL. There was a feeling of sleep in it, a winter's sleep—a grey waiting until spring came. Jerithan lay on his bed, staring up at the fascinating way the thatch crisscrossed itself, the scrunched straws and the ones doubled back on themselves, or the ones dangling right down like little strings and spiderwebs.

He became aware, remotely, that his nose was cold. Unable to pull away from his study of the roof, he wriggled into the blanket until only his eyes were left above it and pushed his jaw out to send the warm breath up to his nose. In—out. In. Out.

He was always colder now that he no longer slept with Kenneth. They had used to be together at night, he and Kenneth on the big wooden bed that had belonged to their parents. Then, one day, Kenneth had brought him in and shown him a new little truckle sort of bed: "Yours, Jerithan. You're getting quite old, big enough for your own bed." Jerithan snorted to himself and turned on his side, burrowing deeper into the blanket. He knew why the bed had been made. Not because he, Jerithan, was getting bigger, but because Kenneth wanted to share the old one with Marianne instead.

He sat up, tossing off the blanket. The cold air washed around him, a curious feeling that he found different from the frigid wind outside: it had cold without movement, or movement so gentle it was hardly movement at all. The sensation was lighter than water, softer than fingers, one that despite the discomfort it caused him, Jerithan liked to analyze.

He glanced over at the sleeping lumps of Kenneth and Marianne in the bed. Grown-up people made such big lumps. He liked to look at their differences: Kenneth's shape was squared and long, more like a box under the coverlet. Marianne was smaller and rounded, like soft hills, and she often slept curled on her side, whereas Kenneth would stretch out flat on his back.

Although he felt a slight resentment towards Marianne for taking his bed, Jerithan minded them both less when they were asleep. It was when they were awake that they acted irritating, like staring at each other during meals, giggling without any rationale, forgetting he was there. And when Kenneth took Marianne's face in both hands and kissed it.

Jerithan made a face and swung his legs over the bed, shoving his feet into his shoes. He paced quietly across the floor and found some bread sitting in the small cupboard, tore off a fair chunk, and ate it. Picking up his coat where it lay by the banked fire, he headed for the door. Kenneth disapproved of him wandering around, but he was bored, bored crazy in this house all day with no one but Marianne.

Carefully he opened the door; hardly a squeak sounded in the icy dawn air as he shut it behind him.

He walked fast at first, making certain to get the house well behind him before Kenneth woke up. But after a little, he stopped in order to decide which way to go. The idea of merely walking, wandering over the mountainside, he scorned. That would be boring, not to mention pointless—and he had left for the whole point of avoiding boredom.

No, he must have something to do. A mile away were the Kings, and Filian King was an interesting companion, even if he were twelve, which was twice Jerithan's age.

The Earles were fun to visit, because they had so many animals—horses, a cow, and chickens, and Jerithan liked to be around animals. They were fascinating to watch and didn't care what you said to them. But then there were the Staffords, who lived closer, and they had animals, too.

Jerithan set his steps towards the Staffords' house.

By the time he reached it, the sun had been up for an hour, and the snow was blazing white on all sides. Lowell Stafford, the youngest boy, near Jerithan's age, was coming out of the barn.

"Hello," Jerithan greeted him, disposed to feel civil towards everyone today.

Lowell, whom Jerithan had snubbed at Kenneth's wedding and who had clearly not forgotten, glowered at Jerithan and walked up to the house without answering.

Jerithan shrugged and followed him in. Inside was delightfully warm, a welcome after an hour's walk. Maira, Lowell's ten-year-old sister, was perched on the edge of a rocking chair by the fire but leaped off when she saw him.

"Jerithan!" she said in surprise. "Mama, Jerithan Denholm is here!"

Kirade Stafford came out of the adjoining kitchen, a stern sort of woman with an angular face that seemed to have lost whatever beauty it once had. It did not much matter to Jerithan, who thought that she was far preferable to someone like Marianne.

She surveyed him now with severe eye. "What brings you here, young lad? Is someone ill?"

"No," said Jerithan. He put his hands thoughtfully into his pockets.

"Only here to visit?"

Jerithan hesitated at this question. "Yes, I suppose so," he said at last, but felt guilty for not telling her the whole truth. She deserved, he was quite sure, to know it.

But, he reasoned, he could not tell her everything. Then he would have to tell her everything, and that would simply take too long.

Mrs. Stafford gave him a brief nod and disappeared into the kitchen again.

"Who did you want to visit with?" Maira asked, settling herself on the rocking chair again and picking up some wool and needles. "Vitty," she added in a quick undertone, "Mama said you were supposed to be knitting, too."

Vitheranel reclined by the fire, her green eyes half-closed and glimmering weirdly in the light like a cat's or a deer's. Her hair curled less than Maira her twin's, and was a color that Mrs. Stafford called dark auburn. Jerithan disliked her, as she maintained a heavy scorn for all children younger than herself and Jerithan was no exception.

"Vitty!" said Maira again.

"I'll do it," said Vitty, making no move to get up. "Later."

Maira gave a huff of her shoulders in exasperation, bright chestnut ringlets flying back. She turned to Jerithan with a clear message of "Let's ignore her," and, clearly happy to talk to him, prattled on for quite a while.

Jerithan found her mildly interesting, but tiresome. He decided there was not much else to do, so he got up, bade Maira farewell, and left the house.

He meant to go to the Earles after that, but halfway there he changed his mind. Although he liked seeing the animals—and sometimes Jared let him ride his great grey stallion, Athlera—Mrs. Earle might ask him how he enjoyed living with Marianne, and Jerithan was not sure how to handle that conversation without turning it into a mess.

No, he would not go the Earles.

So he was shuffling his feet by the side of the road, hating the feeling of having nowhere to be or go, when he heard the brisk footsteps as someone came walking by.

It was a girl, cheeks scarlet in the cold. Jerithan thought he recognized her, though he could not be sure with her face swathed around in a shawl like that. But a wisp of pale hair came flying out to blow in the wind, and then he was almost sure.

Seeing him, she stopped. "H'lo!" she observed and continued to scrutinize him for a little. "You're quite a small boy," she stated, matter-of-factly, and to his own surprise Jerithan liked the way she said it.

"I'm six," he said, "but I will be seven in June."

"I'm going on seventeen," she answered.

"You don't act that old," said Jerithan, having considered for a short time. "My brother's wife is sixteen, too, and you seem younger than her. But that's all right," he added quickly, in case she should misunderstand him. "People act silly when they're grown up."

She stared at him for a moment, and then a grin widened on her face, and she threw her head back and laughed. "I think I must know who you are now," she said. "You're Jerithan Denholm, is that right?"

Jerithan nodded. "You're Sandy Thorne."

"Yes."

They looked curiously at one another.

"You aren't very pretty," said Jerithan. Sandy was not. Her nose was sharp, her jaw sharp and pointed, and her eyes narrow with pale, scant lashes.

"I know," said Sandy. "I haven't ever seen myself very well, but from what I have seen I think I look rather like a cat."

"It doesn't matter," said Jerithan. "You're sensible, and I like you."

She gave him that funny, half-puzzled stare and answered after another short silence. "I like you, too. I think you are one of the most sensible, and honest, people I've ever met."

And there was silence.

"I failed to ask you all this time," said Sandy abruptly, "what are you doing standing by the side of the road like that?"

"Nothing," answered Jerithan.

"Of course. Why, though?"

"I have nothing to do," answered Jerithan.

Sandy pursed her lips meditatively. "Neither do I," she declared. "Let's go up to the castle together. We may find something interesting there."

"Are you sure?" said Jerithan with reluctance. Kenneth would be at the castle by now.

"If nothing else, we'll find people," said Sandy. "And people are always interesting."

~

"An inn," said Lucas Boccin aloud.

Master Boccin had been very thin in his youth: a tall, rangy farrier's apprentice whom Arad Earle's plump, rounded sister had fallen for head-over-heels. Now she was dumpy; he was thickened and somewhat stout. But as she tucked a playful frond of dried rosemary into her silvering bun and shook out the knitted lace on the window curtains, his eyes followed her with warm affection.

"An inn, Lissa," he repeated musingly, running a comb through his hair.

"Lucas, my love, are you dreaming again?"

"There are dreams and dreams, Lissa, my wife; and this is a good dream. Is the castle work not going well?"

"By your account, it is!" She gave him a raised eyebrow over her shoulder. "What of it?"

"By next summer, perhaps, we shall have a lord living there again, and likely more travelers coming up from time to time." Lucas rubbed his thumb along the back of the comb. "A man might get a good deal out of running an inn here, might he not?"

"That he might, if he had a house for it," said his wife pertly, but he saw that he had her interest. "And time to spare from the shoeing that the village needs from him."

"We've a fair-sized house, that might be added onto, and 'tis right in town at that. Gallert is twenty-one, and eager to have his own share of the smithy business."

"A dream, still," said Lissa. "But 'tis a fine dream."

Her husband smiled and stood up to kiss her forehead. "Gallert!" he called.

Gallert appeared in the hall, a tall, handsome young man with his father's thick head of shiny black hair and Lissa's snapping black eyes—though on him, they were languid and disinterested. "Time to leave, Father?"

"Unless we want to miss the whole day's work!" responded Lucas. He laughed and strode with Gallert out the door.

~

Jerithan looked around the castle courtyard with interest. He had been here only once before, months ago before the work started. It had been very quiet then, filled with nothing but cheeping sparrows and chickadees, and everywhere the stones had lain in crumbled ruin. Now it looked strong and strangely beautiful, like something great rearing up towards a still unattained perfection. Jerithan felt, intuitively, that it would still be beautiful when it was finished, but not the same kind of beauty, not the kind that filled it now: the beauty of impetus, of moving forward. All these thoughts filled his head, confused, half-formed in a childish way—yet there.

In his absorption, he had forgotten all the people around him, and Sandy startled him by speaking.

"Ah, there's Bardrick Segelas. He was at our house with his family just a few days ago for dinner. There's Fred," she added and grinned.

"Sandy?" Fred paused by them, covered in a film of stone-dust and looking quite puzzled. "What are you doing here?"

"Standing," replied Sandy. "Watching. What do you think?"

"I see." An answering smile touched Fred's mouth and he moved on with a wave.

"Is he sensible?" asked Jerithan.

"Who? Fred? Oh, yes, Fred is the best man there ever was." Sandy gazed happily after her brother.

"What is going on here?"

The voice made Jerithan turn, surprised for the second time in a minute. It was an unfamiliar voice, and an unfamiliar person as well—very tall, with a lean, clear-cut face that was looking at them both in quizzical amusement.

"Mordred Kenhelm." Sandy gave a saucy bow. "How do you do?"

The smile tilting up the corners of Mordred Kenhelm's mouth widened at this address. "Wondering, as I said, what's going on here."

Mordred Kenhelm, Jerithan knew that name. That was the man Kenneth would mention occasionally, in a tired sort of way, as being "proud" and "difficult to get along with."

"Have you never seen someone stop by and watch the work before?" Sandy retorted.

"I'd say it's out of the common way," Mordred answered.

"Well then, I'll be congratulated as an innovative pioneer, thank you," said Sandy, all complacent seriousness.

"Innovative pioneer it is then," said Mordred with equal gravity. "Or pioneers, since there are two of you." He inclined his head toward Jerithan with another of those laughing half-smiles.

"I'm Jerithan Denholm," said Jerithan.

"Jerithan Denholm? I've met your brother, then. You don't look much like him."

"I know," said Jerithan.

"Yes," said Mordred, looking at him keenly, "I suppose you do."

Jerithan was quite sure that he could ask this person, and he would not get a sharp or condescending answer. "What does that thing that she said, 'innovative pioneer', mean?"

Mordred glanced toward Sandy. "A bold and brilliant genius, more or less."

The definition seemed to please Sandy, who grinned again.

"So," Mordred said, turning directly to Sandy. "I know young Jerithan's name now, and you appear to know mine, but I have no idea who you are."

"I'm Sandy Thorne," replied the same casually. "Fred and Daren's sister."

"Well, Jerithan and Sandy, it has been a pleasure speaking to you," remarked Mordred. "But I must be off to work again, though I am sorry to have to leave your company."

"Kenhelm!" shouted a booming voice across the courtyard. And Mordred whirled about, all the good humor leaching out of his face.

"Aye, sir," he answered, and went swiftly towards the speaker.

"Who yelled?" Jerithan asked.

"I don't know," said Sandy, whose brow was corrugated in a frown. "The foreman, I guess. He seems to be giving orders over there."

"Mordred doesn't like him," said Jerithan.

"Are all children so perceptive?" Sandy wondered aloud.

She was calling him perceptive, which, Jerithan was fairly sure, was a compliment, but she was also talking to herself, which annoyed him.

"Come on," he said, "let's find something interesting to do."

She came out of whatever muse she was in with a jolt. "Of course! Come on."

Jerithan prepared to follow her rapid pace towards the keep, when for the third time a voice spoke behind him, incredulous and sharp.

"Jerithan?"

~

"Mordred, who were you talking to over there?"

Mordred sanded away at the rough edge of the stone, a slight smile hovering around his lips. "A young girl and a boy."

"You seem like you enjoyed it." Therelane was curious, fearfully so, but afraid that if he probed too deeply Mordred would snap closed like a mussel shell.

Mordred flicked a dry look up at Therelane. "They didn't talk to me or look at me like I might bite their heads off," he said. "That was a gratifying change."

Therelane was hurt by the suggestion. "I don't do that, do I, Mordred?"

"Not you. Most other people do. I suppose I've myself only to thank for that," he ended bitterly.

"You don't act that way any longer, Mordred."

"So? They remember that I did, and 'tis all that they remember."

"If they can't see that you are different now, then the fault is in them, not in you." Therelane was surprised by how forcefully the words came out of his mouth—surprised, and almost alarmed. Not often had he ever expressed himself with such vehemence, or, for that matter, had anything vehement to express.

Mordred gave him a small smile. "Thank you for the sympathy, Therelane. But it isn't really necessary. I don't want any friends, and I don't need them either."

He stood up and went to find the rubble cart, leaving Therelane to wonder whether Mordred actually expected him to believe that nonsensical assertion.

~

"Sir?" Kenneth faced the foreman, not caring if his anger were apparent.

The foreman cast a dubious eye over Jerithan standing beside him and grunted an acknowledgment.

"You see my brother wandered out here. He's not supposed to be away from home, and we've no one here to care for him in the meantime; I've got to take him back."

The foreman's eye glinted. "Take him," he rumbled shortly. "And keep your boy in hand after this."

Kenneth bit his lip and pretended he had not heard.

He scolded Jerithan all the way home. All the way home Jerithan remained silent. His face was stolid, as though Kenneth's words were sliding blank and meaningless off his ears.

Kenneth felt frustrated, trapped, betrayed. What had come between them? How was he to make Jerithan respond?

They found Marianne crying when they arrived.

"What's the matter?" Kenneth asked in alarm.

She shook her head, her eyes fastened on Jerithan as she struggled to swallow her tears. "I didn't know where he'd gone—he wasn't in the shed—he didn't come back . . . "

More upset still, Kenneth turned and stared levelly at his younger brother. He could not quite manage to say, "It's your fault: your fault she's crying." Something forbade him to tax Jerithan's young shoulders with that. But he thought it, and he was still thinking it as he turned away and started back to work.

CHAPTER TEN

"**TELL ME TRULY WHAT YOU** think of Fred Thorne, Fiona." Arms crossed, Peony Segelas stared squarely at her younger sister.

Fiona looked up, her eyes widening at the strange confrontation and a blush—oh, how she hated their easy inducement!—sweeping through her cheeks. "What do you mean?"

"What I say." Peony wheeled away to nudge the fire, one hand on a shapely hip and the other wielding the tongs. She straightened again and faced Fiona with a peremptory directness around her sweet mouth. "I'm not accusing you of anything, Fiona; you're my sister, and I think I have a right to know."

"Know what?" Fiona pleaded, bewildered and half afraid that she saw where Peony was going.

"If there is anything between you and Fred Thorne," Peony answered.

Fiona stood very still. For a moment she thought she might cry. "Why would you think that?" she asked in a breathless whisper, her fingers tightening over the edge of the table.

"Because of what you said the other night," said Peony matter-of-factly, shaking out the meal for preparation of the bread dough. "That, and the fact that it's not the first time you've spoken of him, and everyone saw you dancing together at Marianne's wedding. Dear, don't look so horrified. This is not Erahar, and you are not the daughter of a lord. You're at perfect liberty to marry any peasant you like, and

I'm sure that Bardrick won't blink an eye. There, Fiona, now what is wrong?"—for Fiona's chest was heaving, her lip trembling, and as Peony came forward with an attempt at a soothing pat she turned away and ran blindly out the door.

It was too sudden—

So that was what everyone thought. She ought to have realized—but how could even Peony think—

It was too sudden. Fred was the brightest thing in her life, and a man she could not imagine anyone would be opposed to marry. But to her he was still only a dear and beloved friend. She felt no warmth of passion when she saw him, only the warmth of gladness that her heart was so ready to give. She liked him, aye, she could almost say she loved him.

But not as a woman loves a man.

Oh, why did Peony have to speak of it in that way? "Anything between you." It was so blunt, so crude.

She had been so happy with him. And now she felt like she could never be happy with him again.

Another sob caught in Fiona's throat, but she pushed it down this time. She must go back, and she must face Peony without crying.

~

Peony bustled around the kitchen, straightening this and that, and trying and failing to pretend that she was not worried about Fiona.

"The silly girl!" she murmured. "I would give so much to know what she burst into tears for. I didn't mean to upset her, not in the least. And she's gone off without her shawl, besides. My land, she'll freeze to death. If she doesn't come back soon, I'll have to go after her myself."

But not a moment later the door creaked open, and to Peony's relief there was Fiona, her cheeks flushed and tearstained; but her face was composed.

"Fiona!" she exclaimed.

"Peony," said Fiona steadily, "I am not in love with Frederick Thorne. I do not want to hear you say such a thing to me again."

Peony knew she should not look doubtful, but she could not help it.

Fiona regarded her. "Peony, I would not lie to you. You know that. Please do not bring the matter up again, now or ever."

Then, as though she were the older and Peony the younger, she moved with an authoritative air to the table and began to knead the neglected dough.

~

"What did you say?" Braegon cocked his head with a comically astonished grin at Mordred. "You have not been inside the old castle yet?" He shook his head. "A sad deprivation, my friend. Come with me at once; this you must see."

"And what does its inside hold then, save dust and cobwebs, that you desire me to see it so greatly?" Mordred inquired, an answering smile tugging at the corners of his mouth.

"You speak in your ignorance," declaimed Braegon, leading the way to the gaping doorway, "so I will forgive you. But if you found nothing else in here to hold your interest, the library at least would!"

"A library?" repeated Mordred with a glint of interest.

"Aye, that and a marvelous one! How many years it was built up before this place was abandoned, I know not, but it is full of treasures that many a nobleman would pay gold to have. Old manuscripts in Thiredanian and Rodronian, some in other strange tongues, and many in the common tongue as well that speak of conquests, great battles fought by such people as Thireler the Conqueror."

Mordred's eyes were alight. "I would see that," he said. "I learned to read when I was young, before my father and mother died."

Braegon smiled. "I feared, when I took Fred Thorne to see it, that I would never get him away again. I think he would gladly live there and forget to eat or sleep among those piled scrolls."

For a moment Mordred's face cracked into one of those quick laughs, his head tossing up and his face alive in the pale light that fell through high windows. "That is strange, though," he said after a moment, "that there should be so many here. It is such a small place."

"Perhaps," said Braegon. "But Ceristen is strange as well as small. There are the Greys to think of. Once, they say, a strange creature walked the mountain, a shapeshifter of some kind that preyed on men, women, and children. And there may yet be other things that lurk here still; even, perhaps, a wild dragon."

"A dragon?"

~

Braegon's casual declaration that they might be sharing their mountain with a dragon—and not the tame breed, but a true, wild dragon—shocked Mordred and unsettled him to no small extent. But Braegon disregarded his astounded question, saying cheerfully, "Here we are."

He pushed open a half-rotted door that whined in loud protest, and gestured with pride to the room around them, a dim place with parchments tumbled on the floor and the shelves, dust hanging almost visible in the air.

Like the woman's house, Mordred thought in spite of himself. He shook his head firmly, chasing back the willful flicker of memories.

The wind moaned quietly in some outer corridor. Braegon was wandering over the littered floor.

"What are you looking for?" asked Mordred.

"An old carving, a fine rendering in truth. It pictured Haris and his sons in the Great Disobedience."

"The day that death and misery entered the world," said Mordred absently.

"Even so! Three sons were depicted beside Haris himself, and in the framework Holcearor the Dark, who counseled them to seek the well of wisdom in secret."

"It was a fountain that Holcearor told them of," Mordred corrected. "Not a well."

"Was it?" Braegon's shoulders hitched in surprise and easy concession. "I doubt not your word, for you have surely read these things. I myself had heard neither of the Disobedience nor the one who made the worlds before I dwelt here in Ceristen. But it was a well that the artist carved on the stone relief, mistakenly or no."

"A stone relief?" Mordred said.

"And a heavy one—near as long as my arm. It used to lean against the wall, just so, and I thought to show it to you; but it must have been moved. Mayhap Captain Rhodes took it away when he last came." Again, he shrugged and laughed. "Or mayhap I dreamed it."

"A stone relief," repeated Mordred distantly.

"It is no matter," said Braegon. "There is much else to see."

But Mordred saw none of it. He did not even hear much of what Braegon said. A strange, dark feeling drove into his chest like a fishing spear and twisted there, the words echoing in his mind.

"Haris and his sons sought the well of wisdom."

It flashed before him as though he were there again, the dull stone slab with its figures and pillars and trees, the centermost man holding a chalice of the forbidden water to his lips. The still air, the dark panels, and the spiderwebbed halls outside the room of scrolls . . .

Long after Braegon had left, he still stood there, his mouth shut tight on a thousand sinister thoughts, a grim light deep within his eyes.

~

Fenris walked slowly beside his brother, the dusky wine-rose of a winter sunset fading on the rise behind them. Mordred so often was ready to hurry home, though he tried to keep the pace easy for Fenris. But it was not concern for him, Fenris knew, that made Mordred set such a lagging speed this evening. Mordred was walking absently, almost aimlessly, and there was a strange burning look in his eyes.

"Mordred," he said at last with a light touch to his brother's arm.

Mordred stirred and faltered to a stop. "Where are we?" he murmured, staring around.

"At the house," said Fenris. He did not say that they had almost walked past it.

"Ah," said Mordred, a slight satisfaction coloring his voice, as though he had just solved a moderately taxing problem. He turned off the main path onto the little trodden line leading up to the front door.

Supper would have begun and ended in silence if Laufeia had not broken it midway with exasperated tone.

"Mordred," she said. "You are not eating."

Mordred started and looked up. "Aye, so?" he returned brusquely.

"What is the matter? Mordred, did something go wrong at work? Were you fired?" Her gaze flickered from Mordred to Fenris in real alarm.

"Hardly. Enough fearing for me, sister!" Mordred sent his chair skating across the floor and stood up. "I am fine."

Laufeia looked pleadingly at Fenris as their older brother stalked from the room, begging for some answer.

He shook his head. He did not know.

~

"Fenris." Laufeia held him back from following Mordred out into the dim, drippy morning. "Do you know anything of what is possessing him? Anything at all?"

Fenris' soft, worried eyes flew from her to Mordred. "I don't know. He was distracted by something for a few days after he went to look for extra work, but it passed, and he was just as before. But yesterday he went into the castle with Braegon, and when he came out, he wouldn't speak to anyone. There is something bright and hard in his eyes, and all night he tossed without sleeping."

Laufeia shook her head in distress. "I don't know what to do. Stay with him, Fenris. Don't let him wander away alone."

"Aye, Laufeia."

She hesitated, wanting to say more, wanting to tell him her other worry, but afraid to make things worse. And perhaps he already knew that Mordred suffered. That he blamed himself for the scar that Fenris now bore.

"Fenris," she said in a low, earnest voice, touching his shoulder. "Be strong. For his sake."

He looked at her questioningly but nodded. "Aye, Laufeia." And turning, he started after Mordred's dwindling figure in the growing dawn.

~

It was noon in the castle courtyard, and Therelane stood against the outer wall, glancing in perplexity at his friend. Mordred leaned against the stone beside him, an inner tautness in his body and steely shutters across his eyes.

Was Mordred angry, that he had been so quiet these past days? Had he, Therelane, done something against him? Had he—

"Is my face so interesting?"

Therelane stared at him, seeking to probe the toneless question for what lay beneath. "No," he said finally with a sigh.

"Therelane?" His name was uttered softly, tinged with concern. Was Mordred worried about him now?

"What, Mordred?"

"Is something amiss with you?"

He sputtered, the words flying out. "That is what I would ask you, Mordred! You are behaving so strangely. You hardly speak, you seem wrapped in something far away from any of us. Has someone hurt you? What is amiss with you?"

Mordred hesitated, gaze still distant. "I . . . I cannot tell you now, Therelane. Maybe someday. I do not quite know what it is myself, not yet. But you have done nothing to me, nor has anyone else. I will tell you when I can."

Therelane was silent, but Mordred's words did not satisfy him. The look in his eyes was of a man who meant to do something. Whatever he was about to do, Therelane had a sudden frightening premonition that it was dangerous.

CHAPTER ELEVEN

THEY SAT TOGETHER IN THE small, smoky kitchen, Peony busy darning a rip in Bardrick's spare shirt and Fiona mending a worn spot on her own cape. Outside was a fresh, clean morning, and Fiona's eyes ached from the stifled air and the close work; she longed to fling open the windows and let the air in, regardless of the cold.

Peony worked demurely on, no hint on her fair, innocent face that she was inconvenienced by the stuffy atmosphere. With a small, half-concealed sigh, Fiona bent more earnestly over the warm, heavy folds in her lap.

A creak that reached her ear brought her head up with a start, and she saw the door opening on Bardrick and Marcus both.

"Whatever are you doing here?" Peony exclaimed, dropping her work. "It's not yet noon, Bardrick!"

"I am well aware of that, sister," said Bardrick mildly. "As it happens, the thaw yesterday has left a surface of ice over everything in the castle. They sent us all home; it is too dangerous to work today."

"Ah, well; 'tis nothing worse at least." Peony bent to retrieve her sewing. "Are the roads just as bad?"

"No," answered Marcus, "not at all. They were a touch slippery but being already snow-covered the freeze last night did little more than put a fresh crust on them."

"Well then," said Peony, springing up with a vigor that left her previous look of contentment in the dust, "let us get out of this tiresome house and pay the Thornes a neighborly call. 'Twill do us all good to get some fresh air and company for a change."

Fiona's heart leaped at first, and then fell back disconcerted and dulled. See the Thornes? See Fred again? How could she meet his eyes after that day?

She got up quietly and put on the cape and waited for Peony to get herself ready. Begging to stay behind would only bring more questions and looks, and that she did not want.

The walk out in the tingling, sweet air was pleasant despite her unwilling thoughts. She liked to be out with all her family, Marcus making light, jaunty remarks and Peony laughing cluelessly at them, her lovely face looking so happy, and Bardrick striding along, pretending to be too old and wise to be amused but grinning when Marcus could not see. Aye, it was a good walk, and it gave her a certain courage as they approached the house at last, a readiness to face whatever might come.

To her dismay, however, the readiness faded as soon as she entered the door; and when she met Fred's eyes directly across the room, it deserted her altogether. She turned swiftly away and made a long pretense of trying to undo the ties of her cape, and afterwards moved to the edge of the room and stood in the shadows as far from him as she could find. He was, she saw gratefully, busy greeting Bardrick and talking about something else.

The visit dragged out into what seemed an agony. How could they spend so much time talking about nothing? Fiona stood in that shadowy corner, dreading the moment when someone would either notice her or ask after her absence.

Then someone did come towards her. But the someone was Gwenda, and Fiona felt, rather than alarm, a surprising rush of relief. She could talk to Gwenda, she was certain, and if they saw her doing that, surely no one else would bother her.

"Good morning, Gwenda."

"Good morning, Fiona. Why are you all alone?"

I did not take into account her inquisitiveness! I should not have jumped so soon for her company after all.

"I wished to be alone," she answered carefully, "but I do not mind that you came."

Gwenda seemed to contemplate these words a little, but she pressed Fiona no further on it and said instead, "See! I finished the shawl that I showed you before," and she drew out the work in its completion, a simple pattern but executed with neatness.

"It is beautiful." Fiona put an arm around the slender form with a delighted smile. "Beautiful and excellently done! Your sisters taught you well."

Gwenda upturned her shining face to Fiona's and willingly snuggled close against her. Fiona forgot for the moment all her troubles, lost in the joy of being near to someone so small and gentle and vulnerable.

"That is a fair picture indeed," said a voice, startling her out of her contented reverie—a familiar voice, yet one unwelcome to her ear at present. "Were I rich, I would pay an artist all my wealth to see it set down faithfully."

Without lifting her eyes, she answered softly, "That would be a poor gift in place of the real thing before your eyes."

"You go as always to the heart of the matter, my lady Fiona." She heard the gentle smile in his voice. "That is true: it would be."

She said nothing in answer, and when there was silence, she hoped he had gone away; but he spoke again after a moment.

"My lady, you cannot pretend to me. I know you are seeking to avoid my company; is it mine alone you do not want, or that of all?"

She lifted her eyes in a well of surprise, discomposure and candor. "If I seek solitude, it is—yes, it is because I am afraid to encounter you."

"What has happened, then, that makes you so?"

Her gaze fell from his, and she felt the quick color coming. "It is nothing. I am ashamed that I feel so."

"Still, will you not tell me?"

"I—my sister, Peony, discerned our actions together to mean that I was—that I had a woman's love for you." She buried her fiery face in her hands and spoke through the muffling fingers. "So now I am ashamed if we are seen together, lest others think the same."

"My lady Fiona." There was such gentleness in his voice that she felt her face cooling at the simple address, her heart calming. "Let people think and say what they will. If they ask you about it, you will tell them the truth, kindly and honestly. You need not be unsettled by a harmless flight of rumor. Besides, it is only your sister. She may be wont to form conclusions about you quicker than others or sees something and construes from it what she wishes would happen."

Fiona gave a half-laugh in spite of herself. 'Twas true; that was like Peony. "I thank you, Fred. Yet, still . . . I wish it had not happened. We were happy together before, there was nothing between us, but now, this—I cannot explain."

"So, in a sense, there is an innocence removed from our friendship?"

"Aye."

"That is as it must be, my lady. No friendship can stay on the surface forever. It is only when one is willing to speak of deeper things, and ugly things, and unpleasant things, that the friendship can grow firm and true."

Fiona considered his words, and her own thoughts flew through them and murmured themselves aloud. "So we may let it sit between us and grow like a wall—or we may accept that the first sweet edge is gone, and let there be a new openness and honesty that there was not before."

"Aye, my lady."

She met his eyes now without discomfort or shrinking, and a glad smile flowered on her face. "Let it be so, then. I would not grow apart from you."

"Nor I from you, my lady."

~

He looked away from her first, and he let her go to the others; but he watched her as she passed in sure flight from one to another and lent a fresher, purer depth to their companionship.

It had been hard for him to set her at ease, to comfort her in her distress over being thought in love with him, when he was finding himself attracted to her.

~

Jerithan sat by the little window, the only one that boasted a pane of glass, and traced his finger over the frost on it. Circles. Squares. Dots. Lines. It was better than nothing—or was it? Maybe nothing would be better than such pointless employment. Jerithan flopped back onto the floor and listened to the fire crackling.

"Would you like to help me, Jerithan?"

Not Marianne.

"Help with what?" he asked, dragging the words out longer than needed.

"Cooking? I'm making dinner for you and Kenneth right now."

He almost said yes. Cooking didn't sound so bad, after all.

But to do that would be to admit defeat. To admit that he could enjoy himself in the house with Marianne all day. Rebellion rose up in Jerithan at the memory of everything Kenneth had said to him two days before. The ceaseless scolding, saying everything over and over that Jerithan already knew, as if he were stupid. He wouldn't stop talking. And he had said the most hateful, annoying thing of all: "What would your parents say?"

I don't remember my parents. Jerithan rolled furiously on his stomach and stared at the cracks in the boards. *What does it matter what their opinions used to be? How am I supposed to care?*

At first, he had been sorry, or almost sorry, for disobeying. Now he wasn't. And he was determined to be as bored as he could be.

"Are you sure?"

Oh no. Now she was trying to be nice. Jerithan could hear it in her coaxing voice.

"We could have so much fun, Jerithan."

"No," he said stolidly, staring at the floor.

The door banged open. Kenneth? Jerithan looked up in surprise. But it wasn't Kenneth; it was a familiar red-cheeked, snub-nosed face with a braid of pale hair dangling over one shoulder.

"Sandy!" he cried, jumping up.

"Does he know you?" said Marianne in surprise behind him.

"Seems so," remarked Sandy, as though it were a peculiar occurrence. "How do you do, Mrs. Denholm?"

Marianne blushed and giggled in that silly way. "Thank you, Sandy, very well. What brings you here?"

"Oh, naught much. The difficulty is, there's little to do around the house except useful things, and only some people can find an infinite number of those to do." She paused.

"Isabelle can be useful all day long and loves it. Why, she would sleep being useful if she could. I . . . I can only manage what is expected of me, and then my mind rebels and takes me wherever it fancies. Today, Jerithan, it told me it was bored of being inside and watching Isabelle be useful."

"What did it tell you then?" asked Jerithan. He enjoyed the way Sandy talked, such a forthright way of talking, and yet occasionally so roundabout and absurd.

"Why, it told me to come see other bored people."

"How did you know I would be bored?" Jerithan asked, delighted.

"I'm good at guessing," said Sandy.

"So—what will we do now?" Jerithan looked at her expectantly.

"That depends." Sandy glanced at Marianne. "I might just stay here and talk to you . . . or we might go on a walk together. But Marianne would have to say yes to that."

Jerithan felt his cheeks burn. She had been there when Kenneth grabbed him and dragged him out of the castle courtyard. She knew he hadn't been allowed out alone now.

But she still wanted to walk with him—and if only Marianne would say yes . . .

Marianne looked from him to Sandy uncertainly. Jerithan avoided her gaze, unwilling to resort to a pleading expression to get her consent.

She was just opening her mouth to answer when the door banged again. This time, it was Kenneth.

"Too icy for work," he said briefly before Marianne could frame the question. He looked tired and in an ill humor.

Glancing at Sandy, he said, "What's this? Is anything wrong at your house?"

"Oh no," said Sandy easily. "I was just dropping by. Wondered if I could take Jerithan here for a walk, if that's all right with you."

Kenneth frowned. Jerithan could read his face quite plainly. He didn't think Jerithan deserved to take a walk out. He was going to say no.

"He'll be with someone," said Marianne, drawing Kenneth's attention to her. There was some hidden meaning under her words, a plea of sorts on her pretty, freckled face.

Kenneth stared at her, seeming to discern whatever she was trying to convey to him. The resistance faded away and he sighed, looking down at his younger brother. "Go ahead, Jerithan."

And the words were uttered so kindly that Jerithan did not mind rewarding his brother with a happy smile.

Kenneth managed a grin in return. He ruffled Jerithan's hair a little, his brown eyes softening. "Have a good time."

Jerithan nodded as he turned to follow Sandy to the door.

CHAPTER TWELVE

FILIAN STUDIED HIS OLDER BROTHER with thoughtful, alert dark eyes. "Can I come with you, Braegon?"

"Come with me?" Braegon looked at him doubtfully. "You're only twelve, Filian. It's a long and hard day, and one I'm not thinking you could handle yet."

"I'm strong," said Filian.

Braegon smiled. "Strong, aye, but small, like all us Kings are. A bit small yet for a full day's labor at the castle."

Filian sighed and gave him a wry answering smile. "I would like to help though, Braegon."

"I know you would." Braegon touched his brother's arm. "And help you shall, Filian, one of these days—if not at the castle, then at our little farm when the summer comes, and we plant a field. Come, my lad, I know you have patience in you; prove to me that you can wait as well as work."

"I'll prove it, Braegon," Filian answered, throwing his thin young shoulders back with a confident, glad air.

He is such a good boy, thought Braegon as he left the house. Such a strong and brave boy who had been through so much: who never even knew his father, and who had taken the death of the mother he loved so hard.

Braegon's brow furrowed as he remembered those past days, the time when Filian was a boy barely three and their father was called away into the army to serve his time, how four years later the word came back, not that he was coming home, but that he was dead.

"Killed in a skirmish on the north-border with the Wild Men. He bore himself well, Iolaine King; you may honor his memory."

And the time afterwards . . .

Braegon shook his head, his mouth tight. It did no good to think on what lay behind, did he not tell Filian that? But it was harder not to think of it when he had already begun, and when bright-spirited Mirda was not there to turn away his thoughts. Mirda was not like Filian, who approached life with such intense gravity, whom things could hurt very deeply; they hurt her heart, aye, dampened her sunny spirits, but she was quick to rise again. Never did he neglect to assure her that she was the cord that bound their family together.

Braegon smiled a little, and walked on with his light, quick-stepping stride. Other thoughts flitted through his mind, thoughts no longer dwelling in the life behind him, but nearer to the life around him now; thoughts of a tall, grey-eyed young man not a year older than himself, who wrestled alone with a great hurt that was slow to heal, who despite his youth was much more hard a man than one would first assume of him.

We have all become men quicker than we might have. The snowy fields passed away on either side of him, silent, shining bystanders to his sorrowful thoughts. *Perhaps quicker than ought to have been.*

~

Filian sighed.

"Are you tired, Filian?"

He lifted his eyes to Mirda's clear blue ones. "No. Just restless, Mirda."

"Aye, I'm sorry," she said gently.

She must know he was upset inside that his request to Braegon had been turned down, even with his feigned indifference. "It's all right," he said quickly, not wanting her to be distressed for his sake. He was strong, as Braegon had said; he could be a man about this.

She smiled at him. "You know, Filian, you do not have to grow up so fast! Why do you not go out and spend some time with other young people? Mrs. Stafford has children near your age."

Filian frowned a little. "Maira is really too young; she cannot talk of interesting things, Mirda. And Vitty does not like me."

Mirda laughed, her head and curls flying up with a delighted motion. "Oh, Filian! I love your high tastes. What about Lagola Stafford then? She is older."

"She talks too much," said Filian seriously. "And she always tries to be funny."

Mirda threw her hands in the air, laughing. "Can nothing please you, Filian?"

"I might go see Gwenda," said Filian. "She does not talk too much. She is a very good companion for a girl."

Mirda went into fresh spasms at "for a girl," and Filian watched, sober-faced, though he was not displeased.

At last she quieted and gave his shoulder a pat. "That sounds good to me, Filian. You should go to the Thornes and see Gwenda."

Why do I have such good siblings? Filian contemplated his family. *So many people quarrel with their own all the time or dislike them altogether. I do not deserve them; I am sure that if I were in a cross family I would quickly become as unkind as they were. How did I come to have such wonderful people for my brother and sister?*

~

There was a depth to the air, a wholeness that seemed as if the earth were gently throbbing beneath them for the joy of life. They walked together, in silence; rarely did they speak on their journeys to and from the castle. So it was not the silence itself that worried Fenris, but the quality of it.

Never had Mordred been so quiet, so withdrawn from the world. Not even during the days after the accident. Day after day Fenris watched him, and day after day he grew more concerned, yet he could not find it in him to confront Mordred on the matter. Mordred was the one who took initiative, who asked questions and found things out, and Fenris the one content to follow his lead. He did not know how to even begin by speaking first.

"Good day, Mordred!" Braegon called as their paths converged on the open ground before the castle. "And Fenris," he added with his open, flashing smile. "Look at that!" he continued as they passed under the gate and gestured to the high grey walls rising up around them. "'Tis almost finished—that whole outer wall! There's but the small place on the bulwarks, the placing of the keystone in the side gate, and then the remaining gap above it, and we shall have it completed."

Something stirred in Fenris at that excitement. Braegon's cheer caught in more than one face around them, and responding smiles sprang out.

"Think you that we'll have it done today?" said Kenneth, squinting up at the aforementioned gap above the side gate.

"And why not?" cried Braegon enthusiastically. "We shall."

"To work!" The foreman's gruff shout echoed across the yard. "To it. Move your lazy bones!"

~

Mordred bent to pick up the armload of tools offered to him. Therelane was late, or perhaps not coming, for he missed the familiar presence by the wall, though only in a distant fashion.

Why was the world so full of demands? It was impossible to concentrate on his thoughts and come to any decision when he had so much else to remember. He must be going here, there, doing this, eating that, answering things that people said to him . . . and all this time what he needed was to consider the woman, and the black house, and what he must do now.

~

The horse pawed delicately for footing on the slick snow, breath white and snorting in the air, while her dark-eyed rider kept her under tight guidance, scanning for patches of ice ahead.

The brief thaw had not left the roads very passable, thought Captain Rhodes as he guided his mount to the edge of the road where the snow was less packed. "I ought to have come by dragon," he murmured aloud to her. With a twitch of the reins and knees he urged her up the last of the slope, until they hit the level ground and the grey towers flickered through the trees.

The sharp sing of hooves on stone and the ring of hammers and chisels mingled as he entered the courtyard. The labor was moving on apace, he could see at once; and everywhere were the bent backs and busy hands of men hard at work. More men, he dared to guess, than when he had last been here.

The foreman approached from the east gate with his habitual frown. Captain Rhodes reflected good-naturedly that it was too bad the man seemed to think the routine inspections a slur on his capability.

But before the foreman had reached him, a voice exclaimed nearby, "Captain Rhodes!"

Captain Rhodes swung around, dismounting as he recognized a quiet face and steady brown eyes. "Fred Thorne! How goes it with you since we parted in this courtyard?"

"It goes well," Fred answered. "My sister is now wedded, and we are at peace here. It is, as you said to me, a good place."

Captain Rhodes released a soft breath of satisfaction. "I am glad it has proven so for you, Fred Thorne. Though we knew one another scarce a day, I have oft remembered you, and your remarkable family, and wondered how you fared since we met."

He turned, aware that the foreman had arrived and was waiting impatiently behind him.

"How is it going, Colim?" he asked.

"Good as you might expect." Colim scowled deeper. "Got four more on the crew."

"Good news indeed! And the building moves swiftly, I see—the wall is nearly complete."

"Aye," the man grunted, shrugging off the praise. "I could ask for better workers."

"You could ask for better workers?" Captain Rhodes sighed, and stifled back a laugh. Witnessing the earnest toil around him, he could imagine no men more dedicated.

With a shrug, Colim turned away to direct a few who were sanding the edges of a keystone. Captain Rhodes leaned on his horse and watched the work, acknowledging the occasional greeting sent his way.

One face he did not recognize caught his eye, and he found himself watching the young man with dark hair and a mobile, clear-cut face, and grey eyes that seemed often narrowed in concentration. There was something familiar about him, but what, Captain Rhodes could not place. Whether it were in the whole face, or just one feature; nay, more in certain movements that startled him when he was off his guard. Captain Rhodes shook his head, studying the young face. Who was he a reminder of?

"Captain Rhodes, it is so good to see you again!" Braegon King threw him a swift, laughing salute which Captain Rhodes returned obligingly. "So tell me, what are things like now in the great tower of Mitheren?"

"Naught that would interest you, I am sure," answered Captain Rhodes. "I am glad to get out of the talk of alliances and diplomacy to a quiet village like this. You need not envy me my place."

Braegon laughed. "You need not envy me mine either! Every man must work on his home ground. It is only the visitors who think it is relaxing and peaceful."

"True, that." Captain Rhodes grinned as Braegon with a wave hurried off on his own errand.

~

They were ready to put the keystone into place.

It lay by the gate, attached to a makeshift pulley. "Careful of the scaffolding," the foreman ordered as they gathered together, jerking a finger at the rough wooden erections supporting the rest of the arch. "Don't let it swing too much. Two of you, get up there to steady it when it gets high enough."

Jared Earle and Braegon went up onto the wall and waited, small dark figures against the blue sky.

"The rest of you, get by those ropes."

They formed a line and took hold of the ropes trailing over the wooden beam, waiting, listening.

"Ready?" barked the foreman. "Anyone standing on ice? I hope not. Now! Heave!"

~

The stone on the ground wobbled and began to move upwards, swaying crazily in its rude harness. Mordred's gaze followed it as he leaned back on the rope, but his mind was circling back, as ever it did, to the woman, the house, the stolen things.

Why would she have stolen them? What could she gain from it? Surely, if she needed them, if they belonged to her, she might have asked. What reason could she have to hide and steal in secret? Mordred remembered how she had spoken to him that day in such ringing, expectant tones, as though expecting him to be someone else. Who had she thought he was? What kind of visitors did she receive in her black house?

His nose itched, and without thinking he reached up to rub it. The next instant he was grasping frantically for the rope as the whole line of men staggered and swayed at the sudden imbalance in the pull, and the stone dipped wildly, veering for the scaffolding and the arch where Jared and Braegon waited.

"Let go!" the foreman roared.

Instantly eleven pairs of hands released on the rope, and the huge stone plummeted to the ground, landing with a heavy crunch against the scaffolding. The structure shuddered and collapsed in on itself, covering the keystone in a web of twisted boards.

There was sudden utter silence in the courtyard for a short time. Then Lucas Boccin and several others who had been busy loading rubble came hurrying around the keep to see what all the noise had been about.

"There's nobody hurt," the foreman said shortly. "Get back to work." He stalked to the keystone and examined it as best he could with the fallen scaffolding still tangled all over. "Looks like it wasn't marred anyway," he observed. "We'll try again in a minute. For now, start clearing that wood away."

More than a little shaken, Mordred turned aside as Jared and Braegon began climbing down from the wall.

~

"You are both all right?" Mr. Earle reached out and gripped his son's shoulders, looking from him to Braegon.

Jared nodded.

"It never touched us," said Braegon. "You let go of the ropes in time, thankfully, but 'twas a near thing." He bit his lip, his face slightly pale under its dark complexion.

They had not seen it, thought Fenris as he watched them. None of them could have seen it. No one was looking at Mordred—Mordred who was standing, head bowed, by the broken boards, a sick look on his face. They must not have seen the unconscious movement that started it all.

He went swiftly over to his brother. "Mordred."

"Fenris?" Mordred looked up.

Fenris hesitated, looking at his older brother.

"Fenris," said Mordred. "It was my—"

"I know. Mordred, you cannot go on like this. What is the matter with you? Why are you so distracted?"

"You—saw it?"

"Aye, I saw it." Fenris looked up at his brother anxiously. "I do not think anyone else did, but Mordred, you cannot do this! All this past se'ennight and more you have concentrated on nothing but whatever is inside your head. What is going on?"

CHAPTER THIRTEEN

FENRIS' WORDS BROUGHT MORDRED OUT of the distracted daze he had been thinking in for days. He recalled Therelane's similar words to him, considered them with a clearer head. They were truly worried about him. Ought he to tell them what he knew?

But what could he tell? "A woman has taken something from the castle. I suspect she has taken more than that. Then again, perhaps the relief belongs to her. Perhaps not."

Suspect, perhaps; it was all too uncertain. How could they act upon that? They would probably dismiss it as a thing of no matter and advise him against probing further.

No, it would be better to go back to her house alone, to search and find out what he could. When he understood it better, as he had said to Therelane, when he understood it fully, then he could tell them. He would explain it all, and action could be taken.

With that sudden resolve formed, all other confusions and distractions fell away. He knew what he was going to do. It only remained to find out how to do it.

~

Restlessly the thoughts ran around his head, bumping into one another without any clear awareness of what they were or where they were going, trying to think without thinking. It gave him a mind-ache, if such things could exist.

Fred sighed and leaned back in his chair, the fire hissing nearby. What was he thinking about?

Fiona.

Somewhere in all those fragments, that was the only one he could pull back from memory. Fiona Segelas.

"Sandy, I've misplaced my shawl," Isabelle complained.

"You've misplaced it?" Sandy repeated. "Then I don't know what you're looking at me for."

"Are you sure you haven't seen it?"

"I most certainly have not. I don't go around looking at your shawls, Isabelle!"

The house suddenly seemed too loud and confining a place for his mind to stand. He went outside, into the calm, quiet night, to order and consider his thoughts.

It had been her beauty that first struck him: her beauty, her grace, her courteous speech. Yet that fair face, strange as it was, seemed less than nothing to him now. It was but the surface—but the visible reflection of the invisible. When he thought of her, he thought of her intelligence, her quick-seeing heart, her flashes of intuitive reasoning that leaped beyond his careful mind. He thought of the way she lit a room with her thoughtful and yet vivifying words, of the kinship that she could form with any small and helpless thing. Of her endearing hesitancy and the blushes that flew so quickly to her cheeks, evidencing the shy nature beneath; yet so bold she could be when she was at her ease!

He thought of her utter artlessness; of the joy that beamed like a glory from her face when she was glad, a phenomenal light that outshone any other thing in the room, a light that would not fade even when she was eighty and all other beauty had faded from her.

He thought of all these things, and while thinking them, a strong and strange passion seized him that he had never known. Things like it he had known: it was something like the ache he felt when he looked on fair sights, something like the love he felt when he was with his family, but a warmer thing than all of these, a hot and breathless thing that made him quiver with the longing to do a great and reckless deed.

It was so intense for a long moment that he thought he would fly from the ground with its strength. Then it ebbed, ebbed just enough so that he could bear it and think clearly again.

The only conclusion he could reach was that he loved Fiona Segelas. And that thought did not make him sorrowful; rather, it gladdened him beyond anything words could tell. He stared up at the moon, contemplating his gladness, and he might have forgotten himself and stayed in the icy night for hours if Isabelle had not called him in.

~

"There was an accident at work today," Marcus announced with gleaming eyes, shaking the snow violently off his coat like a wet dog.

"Marcus . . . " protested Peony as one soggy lump flew by her ear.

"An accident?" Fiona stood, her brows drawn together in puzzled alarm.

"Nay, not much of an accident," said Bardrick, brushing past Marcus. "No one was hurt."

"Good," said Peony. "I have had enough of accidents this winter."

"There's bound to be more," said Marcus, seating himself with a contented sigh by the fire. "Where there's one, there's more, and I am sure that will hold true of accidents as much as mice."

Peony laughed. Bardrick sent his eyes rolling upwards and said, "There have been two already, Marcus. Or were you so conceited as to forget that you sprained your own ankle?"

"Why, now, did I?" Marcus assumed a shocked expression. "Actually, I must confess 'twas the other one I forgot, Fenris."

Bardrick muttered something inaudible in Eraharian.

"Eh?" said Marcus curiously.

"I was saying," Bardrick observed with deliberate enunciation, "that it is my misfortune to have somehow been cursed with a brother who will face the world's end and still make light of it."

"And mine," said Marcus happily, "to have been cursed with one who can't take a joke."

~

"Fred, why are you smiling?"

"I am smiling?" Fred looked quizzically at Daren, his face breaking out of the soft, light smile that had been hovering over him since breakfast began.

"Yes," said Sandy, who had been about to ask the same question. "Or you were."

"Oh—is it so noticeable?" He smiled awkwardly at them all and gave an uncertain, embarrassed laugh.

The subject went no further, but the following minutes were silent, and Fred was clearly on everyone's mind.

Sandy observed the singular circumstance that he was blushing.

Finally, Fred, with a hurried glance around, stood up and said, "Well, we had better go, Daren."

"What was that about?" Sandy wondered as the door shut behind her brothers.

No answer came; the others were busy cleaning up breakfast now. With a sigh, Sandy dismissed the matter from her thoughts and considered more immediate things, such as how long it would take her to sweep with the broken broom. Or whether she should go see Jerithan Denholm again.

She did find his company delightful, and she was not even sure why. He was simply such a fascinating boy, blunt with a child's tactlessness, yet possessing a curiously analytical mind. Their thought processes and interests coincided more than once, making him still more enjoyable. But, Sandy realized, perhaps what attracted her the most was that he was an unhappy boy—a dissatisfied boy . . .

With a thoughtful, frowning look on her face, Sandy donned her cape and wandered out the door.

Marianne greeted her, smiling, and ushered her in to a chair near the popping fire. "Sandy, how nice to see you again! I'm sorry," she added, seating herself as well, "but Jerithan isn't here today."

"Oh? That's all right, actually," said Sandy, leaning forward to let the heat of the fire envelop her. "I came to talk to you. Where is Jerithan?"

"Oh—" Marianne looked blankly down at her hands. "Kenneth took him with him to work, so that he could make sure someone was keeping an eye on him, he said."

Sandy said nothing. It was not in her nature to be either a quick discerner or an easy comforter; at the same time, she saw plainly that Marianne was less than happy about something. So she asked the only question she could think of in the bluntest way possible. "Do you think he was upset with you?"

Marianne laughed clumsily, like someone trying not to cry. "He—he doesn't feel that I'm capable enough with Jerithan, I think. He's probably right."

"I've never been married before," said Sandy, "but I can guess it's a little bit odd to have your husband making love to you one minute and upbraiding you the next."

"'Tis just . . . " Marianne blinked. "Oh, I sound like a silly girl, but I never expected us to have any—arguments!"

"I don't think it's silly," said Sandy, which was not quite true, because she did think it was silly, but she figured why Marianne might feel that way. "Anyway, he may be more capable with Jerithan, but honestly—" Now it was her turn to hesitate and fumble. The vista she had wanted was wide open before her, a golden opportunity, and suddenly she was not so sure how to word all that had been percolating in her head the past half-hour.

"I don't know how to feel about Jerithan," Marianne said absently, pinching her skirt. "I wish he would let me talk with him, but he refuses to open to me at all. I don't think he even likes me. But he seems to like you."

"He likes frankness. That is what he likes. I am a very frank person, so we get along well together. Neither of us can stand veils or gilding of any kind. But he hasn't learned yet that there's a time for things to stay unsaid, which, I confess, I am still learning myself." She grinned at Marianne. "The strangest thing is people who love frankness can easily hide their own deepest struggles and hurts. After spending time with him, Marianne, I think what he wants is to be loved. Little children don't usually think about whether they're loved or not, but something inside of him is growing unsure. And it's not good." She bit her lip, embarrassed now, and doubtful that she was expressing what she meant.

"What do you mean?" Marianne asked, tilting her head earnestly to the side so that her green eyes met Sandy's.

"I know a girl who wanted to be loved once." Sandy hesitated. "It can grow to an . . . obsession, or worse. Just make sure he knows he's loved."

Marianne was nodding, her freckled face quite sober. "Thank you, Sandy."

"And, Marianne?" Sandy frowned, wondering how to put it. "Kenneth . . . does Kenneth often take himself out on Jerithan?"

"You don't mean—physically?" Marianne looked more than a little horrified.

"No!" gasped Sandy. "Goodness, no! I meant, if he comes home tired, is he likely to be sharp with Jerithan? Scold him?"

"Oh, well . . . yes. He wants Jerithan to grow up, and Jerithan seems to aggravate him more and more lately by being unresponsive, even disobedient—"

"The tighter he confines him, the angrier Jerithan is going to get," said Sandy simply. "And the more uncertain that will make Jerithan, which will make him angrier still. Tell Kenneth he's got to show Jerithan he loves him—at least as much as he disciplines him. Probably more."

"Kenneth does love Jerithan."

"Of course, he does. I don't doubt it. He just needs to realize how his actions appear to him." Sandy got up. "Thanks for the hospitality, Mrs. Denholm. Now if you'll excuse me, I forgot to contribute to the housework this morning and I have to go apologize to Isabelle for shirking my duties." With a roll of her eyes she waved and walked out the door.

~

"Fiona!"

The horrified shriek brought Fiona flying into the kitchen with the expectation that Peony had found a rat in the flour, or some such thing.

"Bardrick and Marcus left their food behind," Peony exclaimed, pointing to the parcel on the table. "They won't have a bite to eat till nightfall!"

"Oh," said Fiona tiredly, a little irked at her sister's panic over such a reparable mishap. "I'm sure no one would let them go hungry, Peony. Besides, 'tis not half noon yet. I can walk to the castle and bring it to them."

So she found herself out on the path, amid whirling, dancing flakes of snow and skies feathery with the tumbling whiteness. It was still with the muffled stillness of snowfall, a silence almost dead and yet not quite complete enough for that: a silence that made a sound without sound, a song of quietude. The thick flakes clumped as large as her fingernails and brushed her nose; her steps faltered, arrested by the beauty happening on every side. Oh—to be alive on a day like this . . .

She ran, skipping, dancing, the snow spraying under her feet and fluttering against her cheeks. The miles slipped away with the moments, and without warning she found her feet come to a stop, nor did she understand why.

And then she knew.

It was the stretch where she had met the woman on the road, the strange shadow woman who had fled the moment their eyes met. A dream, a fancy, she had told herself ever since that day, and she tried to tell herself the same now. But now, standing in the very place, the memory overtaking her coldly, she knew it had not been a dream.

She pulled herself back to the quiet, grey day and walked on. There was no reason to fret over it, no reason to think of it at all.

But the memory lingered with her all the way to the castle.

~

Its massiveness and its grandeur struck her as she stood before it. She had not been so near a castle since the night they left Erahar, and theirs, she was almost sure, had not been this large. Slowly she walked into the gaping mouth of the gate.

"Fiona?" Her brother's incredulous shout must have reached the ears of the entire courtyard. "What are you—oh."

She could not restrain a smile as Marcus paused and regarded the bundle she was offering with a look of studied solemnity.

"It appears we forgot our dinner," he remarked, putting out a hand gravely to take it. "I shall have to tell Bardrick. A thousand thank-yous, sister." And he bowed deeply from the waist, sauntering away with the parcel in hand.

Fiona watched him go, the smile hovering over her lips at his absurd behavior.

She found herself unwilling to go yet, now that she was here and could see all the work ongoing to make this old ruin into a castle again. She glimpsed Marcus again, on his way to join Bardrick by the far wall. A resounding crack drew her attention to Mordred Kenhelm, dark hair hanging in an unruly forelock over his head, swinging a pick into the stone at his feet. Close at hand was Fenris boring another stone, and against the wall stood a young man she did not recognize, watching Mordred.

Mordred turned to him and said briefly, "Get back a little, Therelane. The chips will cut you."

Therelane stepped further to the side, but his eyes followed Mordred with a dissatisfied, even anxious look.

A rattling sound drew her attention away, and she looked to see Fred Thorne pushing a wheelbarrow full of stone fragments and broken bits of wood. He caught sight of her at almost the same moment and checked visibly, his gaze holding hers with an intensity that astonished her and made her look away.

"Fiona." He was hurrying towards her. "Did I startle you?"

She looked at him and laughed. "I think I startled you. For I was expecting to see you here, but you hardly thought to see me."

"True, that. I was somewhat startled." Again, he looked at her in that odd way, though it was more subdued. "But you were glad to see me, I hope?"

"Aye," she answered, staring at him and wondering. That look was so tender, so loving, that it sent a strange thrill and shiver through her heart. "I am always glad to see you, Fred Thorne."

He took a deep, long breath and smiled down at her. "That I am glad of. I hope it will never change, my lady Fiona."

She was not so naive that she did not realize his attitude was out of the common. Her thoughts tumbled confusedly about one another as she left and hurried down through the blowing snow, too confused for her to try to sort them. Maybe there was an inkling, for an instant—

But when she came home, there was dinner to prepare, and Peony vigorously recounting a morning's visit from Marianne, and water to be heated for scrubbing the smoke-greasy walls. She did not think of Fred again.

CHAPTER FOURTEEN

WHEN COULD HE GO?

The wind blew cutting and angry against Mordred's cheek. He scarcely felt it, or the sharp, tiny flakes striking painfully on his face.

When could he go again? Not the break at noon; that was over and gone in the time it took him to walk to the black house and back. Too short a time for him to discover what he needed.

But at night, no one would miss him, and he would be back before morning . . .

At the moon's rising he took his coat and boots, a flint, and the long knife that he had carried ever since their flight from the orphanage and left the house.

The snow, falling steadily all day, had ceased, leaving the bitter, silent cold of winter-death. The moon was full and bright; her pale brilliance threw black spires and strings of shadow across the mountainside. The rises and valleys, clad in their hard, gleaming shell of snow, were girdled with the thin dark bands. Yet Mordred gave none of it more than a passing glance. His mind was bent on the task that he had set himself.

He came upon the house sooner than he had expected, its walls lowering over him, a dark, ruthless hole in the night. For an instant he shrank back from it, buried childish fears rearing in answer to those eyeless windows and menacing towers. Then, tilting his chin arrogantly, he tossed his shoulders back and strode forward under the misting sky, into the shadow.

The silence in the walls overwhelmed him, a deader thing even than the mountain under the moon. Tauter than a horse that smells a snake, he moved forward, groping for the wall and the dusty, unused brackets. His fingers brushed a rough twiggy bundle and closed around it; the dry wood lit in an instant, and he slid the flint back into his coat.

He nudged the door to with a light kick, shining the torch on the hall ahead. The long, milky strands of cobweb fluttered slowly upward with the wind of his movements, caught and clung to him as he passed.

He thought he would never find the room of scrolls.

It was not lighted this time, and his torch threw up wild shadows when he pushed the door open. He replaced one of the dead lights in the brackets with his own and turned, searching.

It was just where he had last seen it, in plain view among the scrolls, the dim fire-glow glancing tentatively off its raised surfaces. Mordred knelt in front of the stone relief and traced his fingers over the ancient, blurred figures. The foremost, water flying spectacularly out of the vessel in his hands, his features locked in an eternal moment of greed and fear; the four others crowding behind him, and the fifth lurking in the frame, carved out instead of raised so as to appear in shadow.

Not a dream. Not removed by some captain. Only waiting, entombed in dark woodwork and spiderwebbed halls, for whatever purpose the strange woman had stolen them away.

Mordred raised his head, taking in the rest of the cluttered room, wondering how much else—all of it?—this woman had taken from the castle.

Why did she steal them?

Why is she here?

He picked up one parchment after another, scanning their contents, even those written in languages he could not read.

What am I looking for?

I do not know. Something, anything that could give an explanation. Why did she take them? If they belonged to her, she could have asked. She would have asked.

Anger stirred up in him at her, at her deceit, at her thievery.

Why?

Scroll after scroll he tossed aside. He picked up the signet ring he had seen, trying to decipher the faded seal and the script scrawled along its outer rim. He glimpsed the ornamental dagger, its elegant hilt rusted almost completely to its sheath. He sifted through a stack of heavy clay tablets, scratched with strange, jagged signs and depictions of bird-like creatures, some of whom bore human features. Across the base of one, someone had inscribed in ink: *Tharen ha i Thangrissere.*

"Who comes as a thief and invader into my house?"

Mordred sprang to his feet with a stifled cry.

They stared at one another, still as the stone carving on the floor between them, silence rushing past like a suffocating tide.

Then Mordred spoke.

"You took them," he said softly.

She did not answer.

"Do you deny it?" he asked her, cold, accusing.

"I do not deny it." She stood tall and angry in the door, her arms outstretched in a gesture of scorn. And then Mordred was afraid, for he knew that she would not let him go.

He took a slow step to the side, sliding his knife with the smallest of rings from its sheath.

Her eyes flicked to the blade, and her lip curled up in a sneer. “You will not get away by that,” she said; and with a lithe movement she reached up and snatched a long sword from where it had been resting on the wall.

She meant to kill him—

Mordred knew a more blinding fear than he had ever in his life as he watched her come towards him, a fear that made his heart thunder like an erratic wingbeat and his vision dim. But the fear, strangely, lasted only moments. A cold, disinterested calm flashed into its place.

Let her come, then. She shall not see me tremble.

He flung up his head as she approached, a faint, detached return of that old sense of recklessness goading a small smile to his lips. He saw the ease and familiarity with which she held the sword, and knew, with that keen detachment, that it would be no use to fend her off with his inexperience and skinning knife. So he tossed it disdainfully away.

She halted just beyond arm’s length, surveying him, looking almost puzzled. For an instant he thought of rushing past her, out the door, and fierce hope lurched up through the cool daze surrounding him. The next instant, the sword was swinging at his head.

As he fell in a daze of pain and sinking blackness, he felt a sudden sharp sting of grief, and of regret: *Fenris . . .*

~

“Where is he?” Laufeia muttered, meaning specifically Mordred, though in her head she was referring to both her brothers. However, she had no doubt in her head that Mordred was the one responsible for neither appearing at breakfast yet.

She cast a vexed look at the steaming pot. If they thought they were going to eat cold porridge, they could think again. With a quick motion she leaped up and started for the bedroom.

Fenris came out just before she reached it. "Mordred is gone," he said.

Laufeia pinched her lips together in rising annoyance. "Gone already? What does he think he is made of? I don't think he knows what he's doing these days anymore! Fenris, take some food with you and see if you can catch up to him before he reaches the castle. My land, do I have to care for my own older brother like a baby?"

Fenris did not move toward the kitchen. His eyes were turned away from hers, dark and troubled. "Do you think he is—"

"Fenris, don't worry," Laufeia cut in impatiently. "He'll be fine if you can get some food into him. Hurry up and eat now so you can leave."

Fenris said no more but obeyed quietly. The door closed behind him in a matter of minutes, leaving Laufeia alone with her thoughts and a vague sense of unease.

She moved about the kitchen, restless, wandering back and forth. She tried to wash the living-room walls but could not focus. An hour waned away, the sun fully risen and climbing towards noon, before she broke away at last from her futile attempts at housework. It was no good; she must get out, maybe visit someone—Mirda?

And so, she pulled on her shoes, stepped into the crisp air, and set off for the Kings.

"Laufeia!" Mirda greeted her with a prompt smile and a warm embrace.

They sat down at the hearth and talked of little things, such as how quickly the days sped and how long it might be until the castle was finished; they played with one another's hair laughingly, Laufeia coiling Mirda's springy dark curls behind her head, Mirda's fingers twisting Laufeia's long hair into elegant braids.

"Look how Filian is growing," Mirda exclaimed with a gesture to Filian, who backed into the corner, peering at them from under his dark sweep of hair, and she laughed again with Laufeia.

And the whole time, the nagging feeling remained in the back of Laufeia's mind, all the more unpleasant for its lack of definition and form.

At last she bade Mirda farewell and started for home again.

She stepped into the dark, warm kitchen, smelling the smoke and lingering aroma of the breakfast porridge. The little whisk broom leaned against the wall, and she picked it up, reflecting wearily that it was time she got some sort of work done.

"Laufeia?"

She whirled, startled. Fenris was in the doorway. "What on earth?"

Fenris wet his lips, struggled to speak. "Mordred was not at the castle."

She heard him in silence. Into the silence spoke her own voice, exacting calm, refusing to worry yet. "Have you looked for him?"

"A little."

"Does anyone else know?"

"Braegon and the others. He said that if I did not find him soon, to tell them."

That steady, clear voice was still speaking out of her. Another part was crying in terror, *No! No, I cannot go through this again.* "Where have you looked?"

"I retraced the path back to the house, looking for any footprints leading off it—that is all."

"He might have gone somewhere in the night." The instant the words left her mouth, she wished she had not said them, wished she had left them to remain blank and unspoken in the depths of her mind.

"Something woke me in the night." She could see how hard Fenris was striving to steady his voice. "I thought it was the wind rattling the house. It might have been him leaving."

Oh, Fenris. He must not blame himself for not knowing, for not looking. She stepped up to him and gathered him in a tight, quick hug. "We will find him, Fenris."

But she was afraid, almost as afraid as when Fenris had gone missing near a month ago. Maybe more. While not as strong as his brother, Fenris was by far the steadier; he had never been one to rush into foolishness. Mordred, on the other hand, attracted danger like the plague. If Fenris' inadvertent disappearance had ended in such disaster, then what would Mordred's deliberate departure by night bring? *What* could he have planned to do? Dread curled sickeningly in her chest.

Still she refused to let her mind believe. She must keep hold on herself, must not panic yet. "You'd best go back to the castle, Fenris, and let them know."

He nodded a little and turned to walk quickly down the road.

~

"Fenris!" Braegon dropped his lever and pry bar and sped to the lone figure coming into the gate. "Nothing?"

The other men around them slacked their own work, waiting.

"I don't think he ever slept last night," said Fenris, his words scarcely audible even to Braegon beside him. "I do not know where he would have gone."

"Maybe we can find traces," said Braegon. "Footprints."

"Not likely." It was Mr. Earle coming forward with quiet step. "It snowed sometime in the night. Still, we can look."

"You all want to shirk your duty for a missing man again?" shouted the foreman, storming toward them. "What am I supposed to tell Captain Rhodes next time he comes here and wants to see progress? Shall I have none at all to show for him?"

"There now," Braegon began steadily, "no one mentioned searching right now, sir."

"I'll search now," said Therelane, stepping forward. There was a certain steel behind his anxious grey eyes.

"And I," said, surprisingly, Kenneth.

Fred came out. "And I, sir."

There was an odd silence.

"I, too, sir," said Bardrick. And Marcus at once piped up:

"Where Bardrick goes, I am certainly going as well."

"Sir," said Mr. Earle to the infuriated foreman, "we are far ahead of schedule. You cannot grudge one day to return a man to his family."

"I'll grudge it all right," snapped the foreman, "but I will give it to you. Why you're all set on looking for him, I don't know. He was the worst man of the crew and he was uncivil to each and every one of you."

"That's in the past," said Braegon grimly. Long had he borne with the foreman, but this was going too far. "It's been a fortnight and more since he spoke any word of discourtesy to you, sir, much less another one of us. You have ill-used him, and I've done with it. What he's suffered under is more than any man of eighteen should have to, and there's many a grown man who wouldn't have come out the better for it, and all you can see is the enmity that you should have put behind you long ago."

The foreman started for a blustering reply, but Braegon overrode him. "However long it takes me to find Mordred Kenhelm, sir, I shall look until I do. And if I ever hear you treating him in that manner again, I will not work under you another day."

And the men who not long since had disliked and shunned Mordred Kenhelm united in the face of despite and anger to search for him, even as they had searched for Fenris weeks ago.

CHAPTER FIFTEEN

THEY SPLIT INTO FOUR GROUPS: Braegon, the Thornes and Fenris in one; Lucas Boccin, Mr. Earle, and their sons in the second; Kenneth Denholm, Therelane and Edrach Stafford in the third; and Julius Mogra, Charles Delaney, and the Segelas brothers in the last. They agreed to regroup to the King's house, and if anyone found traces, he was to report back there and sound the horn call for the others to return.

Braegon struck out east, motioning for the others to follow him. They entered the woods, fanned out and doubled back again, looking under every low-lying pine bough and behind the high banks of snow. And every now and again one of them raised a call, echoed more faintly by those of the other groups in the distance. "Mordred! . . . Mordred!"

Down a steep hill Braegon threaded his way, glancing up and down the sharp gulch. The snow collected at the bottom in deep drifts, and he ploughed through the length of it, searching for any dark spot or broken surface to the clean, soft whiteness.

"Braegon!" Daren called from the top of the ravine. "Are you all right down there?"

"Aye," he called back.

"Don't get separated."

The first hope, the first quick energy, was good for all of them. They covered ground rapidly, looking here and there with eager speed, calling comradely words of encouragement to one another. But miles passed over miles without a trace, and weariness crept in under their spirits. They no longer thought to find him soon.

But not one of them turned back. The core of their searching was now laid bare, fierce and red-hot and unquenchable: to search and find no matter the effort and cost. Find him they must; find him they would. And so, weary, disillusioned, but resolute, they searched on.

Braegon's party broke out unexpectedly onto the road again. In the feeling of clear air and openness, they paused to take a breather.

"What is that?" Fred asked, pointing down the little trail leading off the road and the edge of a house faintly visible at the end of it.

"That's the empty old Grey's house," said Braegon. He heaved himself up off the ground, his shoulders sagging with exhaustion. "Come, let's move on."

~

Laufeia moved mindlessly over the floor, cold all through and frantic with the waiting. She caught herself and stopped beside the fireplace, twisting her icy hands together. How long had it been since Fenris left? An hour? She must stop fretting, stop wondering—it was less than useless. 'Twould do no one any good.

She walked briskly to the bedroom, took all the blankets they had, and piled them up by the fire, which she built up until it was roaring high. She took a few strips of cloth and set them soaking in a pail of water and got out a little tub of greasy ointment-stuff; Mrs. Stafford had given it to them a fortnight past, saying it was good for injuries. So Laufeia placed it by the bandages and boiled up what was left of the herbs that they had used for Fenris. Strangely, the actions of preparing for an accident steadied her. It seemed to say that they would find Mordred, and she could be ready for whatever contingency there were. She was calm again.

Noon came and went while she was busy, and only the murmuring in her stomach reminded her towards midafternoon that she had not eaten for eight hours. She sat down and made something of a belated dinner, but her appetite was wan and easily satisfied. Up she rose again and began to prepare supper for when Fenris might return. Darkness fell.

A knock at the door sent her running to answer, and it was Braegon there, looking weary to the bone. “I'm sorry, Laufeia,” he said, looking down and away from her. “We couldn't find him. We'll look again tomorrow.”

Laufeia nodded. She did not feel the blow she had expected. All she felt was the frustration for all that time she had spent making preparations, now pointless.

Fenris came forward under the doorway as Braegon turned into the darkness. Laufeia thought that the tears would come then, watching him, so tired, so young, so alone. Fenris had never seemed the older to her, but the younger, even from the days before the orphanage; he always had, and he still did, and her woman's heart ached for him.

He did not notice her long gaze but walked dazedly past her and sat down at the table where she had set his plate. He made no move to eat, only sat motionless for so long that she feared she might have to coax him. But in the end, he did.

~

“Braegon?” Filian looked at his brother, who was slumped back in a chair beside the fire, a wool cap lying across his eyes. He spoke quickly, earnestly. “Braegon, can I please help to search tomorrow?”

Mirda, in the corner knitting, looked up. "Oh, Filian, don't you think—"

Braegon pushed the cap back. His tired voice cut into Mirda's, brusque, hard. "Yes, Filian. We need every man we can get out there."

~

Marcus came home, limping.

In-between Bardrick's brief, muttered explanations of what had been going on, Fiona and Peony gathered that Marcus had twisted his ankle—the same one that he had sprained before—stepping into a foxhole that had been covered by snow. He had insisted it was mild enough to keep on searching, although Bardrick had suggested bringing him home, and so he had driven himself on it all afternoon.

"Well," Marcus explained weakly, "it felt better earlier."

"You should have told me when it got worse," said Bardrick with less exasperation than concern as he looked at his brother's white face.

"But I was too proud to tell you I had changed my mind," said Marcus with a wry grin. "It's the problem of having an older brother."

"You're not coming with me tomorrow," said Bardrick. "I don't want to see you stepping on that foot for another day at least. And after this, for pity's sake watch out for foxholes."

He turned around and left the room.

"I couldn't have seen the hole," protested Marcus plaintively. "No one could have."

"Tomorrow," repeated Fiona. "So you did not find him?"

Marcus shook his head, his eyelids drifting closed. "No—and Bardrick's taking it hard. We all are . . . "

His voice murmured away sleepily. His lashes flickered once and rested dark on his pale face as his hand loosed Fiona's and he slept.

~

Marcus' ankle was swollen from the pressure that he had placed on it for hours, and he slept restlessly that night. Fiona stayed close beside him, putting warm poultices on the ankle, coaxing him to take a sip of tea, and catching the odd moment of sleep while he was quiet. To her great relief, he showed no sign of growing feverish. For the most part he was drowsy, but occasionally he seemed more wakeful, and would tease her about being such a lady of mercy as to stay up with him all night long.

"Fiona," he remarked in one of those lively moods, "I declare, you ought to come visit the castle more often."

"Why?" she asked, knowing there was more explanation to come.

"I get so much more attention when you do. Gallert Boccin came up to me and asked with a flatteringly assumed air of disinterest why I hadn't told him what a fair sister I had, and whether she were promised."

"Marcus!" she cried in horror.

"Oh, I told him off when he said that. Said that no, you weren't, but Bardrick was very picky about who came hanging around his sisters, and after all, we were nobility, and he seemed rather crestfallen but didn't address the matter again."

"Marcus!" She could have slapped him.

"And then the foreman asked me whether that pretty little thing were my sister, and I said yes, and he said she'd better get her pretty little face out before it got crushed by another falling stone. First I've seen for him to be concerned for anyone's welfare." He grinned at her appalled face. "Fred was the only one who asked the sensible question of why you were there at all."

"Fred?" She did not know why she blushed and was glad the candle-light was so dim.

"Oh yes. He seemed quite surprised that you were there." Marcus yawned and relaxed against the pillow. "Certainly not sorry to see you, just surprised."

Her thoughts were fluttering like mad birds, her heart quivering and warm—where was the sense in it? Where was the reason? Marcus had not said anything odd, not even anything she did not already know.

"Fiona?" Marcus' eyes were trained steadily on her. "Do you know what you feel about Fred, sister?"

She could not make sense out of anything. "I—I do not know."

"I think Fred fancies you, *eghuire*." At his soft use of the Eraharian word, their birth tongue, the tears started behind her eyes. "Whatever you are feeling, you had better figure it out soon."

One tear spilled over and fell onto his hand. He reached out and rubbed her wrist lightly. "I know, *eghuire*, you feel confused. You hate the decisions when you aren't even sure of your own mind. Don't cry. It will look better in the morning."

Wait until morning when her heart was in such a turmoil? She could not so much as shut her eyes, let alone sleep. *What do I know? What do I feel? What am I?*

Until now she had steadfastly considered Fred a friend and had been happy to give him all the generous love and comradeship her heart could hold, no more or less than she did any other. But now, this: this spinning of heart and head, this heat spreading through her body—was it only an empty response to the suggestion that *he* might love *her*, or was it more? Had her friendship taken another road?

I would have to see him again before I know. Before I can say anything.

The candle flickered low. Marcus slept. Fiona sat with burning eyes beside him, watching the flame ebb into a spark, and then nothing.

~

They all met at Braegon's house, rested with a night's sleep and grim-faced, ready for another day of searching.

"We covered most of the south slope yesterday," said Braegon. "Mr. Earle, your men can do another brief check of that. The rest of us will move on to the west side."

Mr. Earle nodded.

"Filian, you'll come with my group." Braegon put an arm firmly around his younger brother's shoulders as Filian pushed eagerly to his side.

He glanced around the waiting faces. "Come, then, let's go."

~

"You've been caring for him through the night, dear," said Peony, taking Fiona's hand and pulling her out of the chair. "I'll take a turn. Why don't you rest?"

"I am not tired." She was not tired; well, maybe tired, but not sleepy. There was too much in her head, and she needed to do something to calm it. "I think I will go see Laufeia."

"Well, if you are sure you don't need to sleep. Poor girl, she's having a hard time, I don't doubt." Peony clucked over either Marcus or Laufeia and began examining Marcus' ankle. "Good, the swelling's going down . . . "

Fiona walked swiftly through the clear morning and reached the Kenhelms' house in less than an hour. Laufeia solemnly answered her knock, and there the two girls stood, simply looking at one another for a moment. Then Laufeia's lip trembled, and though she bit it hard she could not stop the tears that came streaming down her cheeks.

Fiona took a quick step forward and held out her arms, gathering Laufeia into a tight embrace. Her heart was trembling with grief and compassion, wrung for the other girl who was enduring so much. Her tears mingled with Laufeia's.

At last they drew apart. There was no awkwardness between them, no false face to reassume. Their first meeting had happened in the midst of utter vulnerability, and they had no need to be ashamed of breaking.

"When did you find him missing?" Fiona asked as they sat down together.

"Fenris told me he was gone at breakfast. I think he may have realized something was amiss, but I brushed it off; I thought he had only gone on ahead. He has been so absent-minded lately, Fiona." Her eyes lifted to Fiona's, anxious, filled with dread. "I cannot bear to imagine what could have happened to him. I—I fear he must have been going mad. Ai, it sounds so silly, but what would drive him from the house in the middle of the night? And when he is absent-minded like that, he does such foolish things. He might walk off a cliff without noticing. Maybe he did." She clamped her lips shut, as though that had escaped without her meaning.

Fiona closed her hands tightly around Laufeia's. "Nay, Laufeia. They will find him. Do not fear."

Laufeia only managed the barest trace of a smile. Her eyes gazed down at the bare darkness of the dirt floor.

~

Twilight was closing in on them. Slow, crunching footsteps sounded as Braegon's group wandered over the snow. *No . . . use . . .* they seemed to say. *No . . . use . . . no . . . use . . .*

Braegon halted and turned to look at all of them. "Time to head back," he said.

He saw their faces slacken; their bodies slumped despondently. But it was Fenris that his eyes sought, Fenris who had not spoken one word yet this day.

A shudder, almost invisible, went through the boy's form. But he held himself as straight and still as before. His dark eyes were bleak, quiet, locked in an almost fierce resolve.

Why—he has steel in him, too. Braegon checked a moment, studying and measuring the young lad with new eyes.

Unconsciously, their steps drew them to the Kenhelm house, rather than Braegon's where they had been supposed to meet first and reaching it they found that the other groups had also come there, by unspoken compulsion.

Scarcely had they glanced in surprise at one another when Laufeia suddenly opened the door and looked out at them. Not one of them was willing to meet her gaze, so they all looked away in a painful silence.

Braegon broke it at last. "We could not find him," he said, and the words tingled on the still air.

A stirring rippled among the men. Then Edrach Stafford raised his voice. "If he was lost out there, there is little reason to hope any longer. He could not have survived two nights out in this cold."

Gallert Boccin added his voice, smooth and regretful. "It would be best to stop now."

Lucas Boccin elbowed his son sharply.

Braegon's glance flashed to Fenris, whose desperate calm of moments before had shattered. He reached out and took the boy's shaking arm in a firm grip. "One more day," he said. "If we don't find him then, let it be called done."

There was a silence again, and one head after another dropped in a nod.

Mr. Earle spoke for them all, as he was wont to do. "So be it," he said. "One more day."

CHAPTER SIXTEEN

DREAMS WERE WRAPPING THEIR NETS around him, tangling him in oblivion, but it was time to wake. He stirred. A sizzling needle of pain raced through his head, and he sucked back the whimper that would have escaped him.

Where? When—

Walking to the black house by night, wandering among the stolen scrolls, caught. The woman had walked toward him with the sword; she had been about to kill him.

But she had not killed him. Then what had happened?

Mordred opened his eyes, and the pain flowered forth again like a band of iron locked around his brow, with a thorn stabbing just above his ear. He bit his lip hard, waiting for it to subside.

The room around him was very dimly lit, and he could not tell where the source was, but it did not seem to come from anywhere in the room itself. The walls around him were stone, as well as the floor under him, he realized. It was small and smelled of apples and fermented barley. A store-room.

So he was not in his own house, and certainly nowhere he had been before. He must still be in the woman's home.

Before his thoughts could get any further, there was a creak like the opening of a door, and footsteps whisked over the stone toward him. A pair of boots entered his vision, a silver-grey skirt swishing just above their toes, and halted before his eyes.

"So, you are finally awake."

"How did you know I was awake?"

"There is an opening in the door," she answered, "which is useful to watch through."

"Why were you watching me?"

A moment of quiet passed. Then she said coldly, "Perhaps I wished to speak with you."

"What do you want with me?" He spoke as coldly as she, with all the inflection of scorn he had.

He felt her hesitation. "I am not quite sure."

"You must want something of me. Why am I here?"

"I could not let you go," she answered sharply. He looked up at her bitter, dark eyes and narrow-set mouth. "I could not let you go, and I was not able to kill you in cold blood, either. Why did you not fight me?"

He scarcely knew himself, and those last moments were a pain-distorted blur in his mind, and so he made no answer—if, indeed, she wanted any. "What do you want with me?" he repeated. "What are you going to do?"

"I will leave you down here, alone, to perish. No one will hear you, no matter how loud you call, nor will they find you, no matter how long they scour the woods."

"Oh, so you could not kill me with a sword, but the slower, more torturous end seems to you more humane?" He threw the words at her scathingly. "Is it blood you fear, woman?"

Her gaze darkened, and he thought she might strike him. "I drew blood from you with that sword," she said softly. "Do not make me do it again. I wish to have no hand in your death, that is all; I will let nature make an end of you. Farewell, bold man," she ended mockingly and turned to walk across the floor again. The door clicked shut behind her.

~

When he was certain she had gone he lunged up, recking nothing of the pangs that seared through his head. He stumbled to the door and felt for the handle, only to find that there was none. An opening—but it was covered in a grid of iron bars. He clenched his hands around them and shook them, shook them, in vain: they would not loosen. He flung himself against the door, again and again, and then his strength gave out and he fell to the floor, helpless under a red sea of pain and nausea.

It was a long time before the agony and sickness abated, but as soon as they had, he began to wish them back again; for while they lasted, there was no room for thought. Now he could think again, and it was more painful than any wound. How long had he been here? They would be looking for him now, surely. Fenris, Laufeia, Braegon. And the woman had been right. They would look everywhere but here. Why would they look in the old house that hardly anyone remembered these days, that was supposed to be empty and alone? They would search woods and Wilds and never find a trace. And Fenris . . .

The tears slipped out of his eyes. Fenris suffering under such a blow—it would crush him. It might kill him. And all for a foolish resolution to solve the problem himself. Why had he told no one? Why? Why?

Mordred buried his face in the cold stone and bit his lip, shut his eyes, trying to keep back the tears, but they fell all the same.

~

Marcus was chafing at the required bed-rest. "Please, Fiona," he begged. "Please don't make me stay behind today. Not the last day of the search! Just suppose if I went, maybe one more person would make the difference—"

She said nothing, knowing that if she even looked at him, his pleading face would be enough to make her cry. She drew the needle carefully through the wool in her hands, spacing the small stitches with painful exactitude.

"Marcus, don't fuss about it," said Peony firmly, bustling in from the kitchen. "Anyway, Bardrick already left, and if you think I'd let you walk to the Kings' on your own you're greatly mistaken."

Marcus flashed her an unusually upset look before shutting his eyes and lying back.

"It's a fine day out," said Peony a little later to Fiona. "I think I will go out and get some air, if you don't mind caring for Marcus?"

Fiona shook her head.

"She already is," said Marcus.

"Marcus," said Peony reproachfully, "are you trying to say I'm being selfish?"

Marcus' mouth curled in a petulant scowl. "Oh, just go on and take your walk."

"Marcus." This time it was Fiona who uttered it in disapproval as the door shut behind Peony.

Marcus gave a half-apologetic shrug and made some kind of light remark to dismiss the subject. Fiona thought to press it, but, knowing that his injury was partly at fault for his irritable behavior, said nothing.

~

The last day.

They must find him today, even if it were only his body. At least that would be a closure, a consolation of some harsh kind. But as Braegon looked from face to face, he saw the doubt and despair there and knew that none of them believed that Mordred would be found. They had spent themselves for two long days, tramping from dawn until nightfall all for nothing. Why would today prove different?

He did not have any faith himself. Maybe Fenris was the only one who did—Fenris with his thin frame held so steady and upright, his eyes full of his last hope. He looked at the boy and dreaded the result if this day should be like the first two. How could Fenris bear the death of the brother he was knit to so strongly?

"Come." He glanced around at his group, the last to leave. "Let's go."

They moved without animation or vigor. Every square foot of snow seemed like the one before it; even the occasional slip or tumble, break as it was from the monotony of useless searching, seemed sluggish.

"Come!" said Braegon suddenly and sharply, when noon had passed, and the sun was just beginning to wester. "If we're going to search, then search! Enough of this gloom. Let's search like we mean to find him. Find him we shall!"

His spirit caught in them all, and they flung themselves into the effort, and hope stirred again in each man. But it flagged again as the sky began to darken and no sign came.

~

"Remember what horrible stories Bardrick used to tell us when we were children?" Marcus waved away the steaming tea that Fiona was bringing to him. "No, please. No more of that watery stuff."

Fiona sighed and set it on the table instead. "Yes, I remember, Marcus."

"The ones about the ogre with a husk for a head and fire that shot out of his fingers?"

"Yes, Marcus."

"And the one about the woman with a white, bony face and a long dark cloak that made night come whenever she swept it across the sky?"

Fiona stirred and turned away a little. "I remember that one."

"What's wrong, Fiona?"

"Naught. It only reminded me of something I saw once."

"You saw the woman with the cloak of night?" Marcus laughed. "Do tell, sister."

"I saw a woman. It was the night of the wedding right after we came here. I was coming home, and she came out of the woods by the path, all swathed in her dark cloak, and then she saw me. And, Marcus, she whirled around like a startled deer and barreled back into the trees! Isn't it odd?"

"It is odd," said Marcus thoughtfully. "It's extraordinary. Why on earth would she do that? Do you know who she was?"

"She was not any woman in the village. Not unless there is one I never heard of."

"Maybe she was a Grey?" Marcus offered. "There are several girls in the family, I hear, and of course the mad ones might be skittish of being seen."

"Maybe." Fiona considered the suggestion and found herself relieved. It seemed much better for it to have been a villager, even a madwoman, rather than some stranger or a phantom of the night. "What are they like?"

"Oh, let me see. I asked Braegon one time. There is Mrs. Grey, but she is not mad and from what he says of her she seems hardly one to be tiptoeing around the forest by night. There is Irene Grey, and she apparently has the power of healing—nay, it's the power of knowing ailments. Braegon said she's small and dark-haired. Does that sound right?"

Fiona shook her head. "She was tall."

"Well, the other girl is Ledelia. She's the oddest one of all, apparently. Goes off her head screaming or wanders around at night, sings sad songs; maybe she's your girl. She is fairly tall, Braegon said, and though she's only twenty her hair is silver."

Fiona blinked and shook her head firmly, her heart sinking in her chest. "She was cloaked, but not hooded. I would have noticed if her hair were silver. It can't be her, Marcus."

"Then who?" Marcus threw her hands in the air. "There's no other Grey women I know of!"

"Then it wasn't a Grey. Oh, Marcus, do you think I imagined her? Do you think I am going mad?"

"No," said Marcus cheerfully. "We've merely got a conundrum, and a very intriguing one. Let's solve it."

Fiona gave a sigh. "All right. Do you know of any other houses in Ceristen?"

"Fiona!" Marcus sat bolt upright.

"Marcus—Marcus—what?"

"I can't believe it," Marcus was saying. "I can't believe it. I can't—Fiona, you're a seer. You're a genius. You're—"

"Marcus!"

"I should have known. Why, it all fits perfectly."

"Marcus, if you do not explain I am going to shake you. What on earth are you saying?"

Marcus took an excited, quivery breath. "I'll try." He suddenly looked unsure of himself. "Maybe I was wrong. It's probably like a dream; it'll look all wrong again in a minute. There is another house in the village, Fiona."

"Oh? So maybe she does live there."

"Maybe she does. That's neither here nor there. But, Fiona, I wouldn't know about the house except that one time at work Mordred asked Braegon, 'Who owns the black house near the castle?' or something like that. And Mr. Earle said it was an old thing built by an ancestor of the Greys. But Mordred couldn't have known about it unless he'd been there."

"He might have only seen it," said Fiona, who still did not understand what Marcus was saying in all this.

Marcus scoffed. "You know nothing of Mordred, Fiona! I've seen enough of him at least to know this: if he saw a big black house, he'd go up and look at it. Next thing you know, he'd be inside. And it explains it all, Fiona! It explains why he's been so distracted lately! He's been obsessed over the house. And of course, he went to see it again, at night because he couldn't explore it during the day."

"Marcus, that is so ridiculously far-fetched—"

Marcus looked a little hurt. "Maybe some of it is guesswork. But it fits, Fiona. We have to at least take a look in that house. I'll warrant you fifty recenna no one has thought to take the littlest peek in it. What harm could it do? None. And maybe he's in there."

"Maybe," said Fiona softly. Her head spun, trying to absorb what Marcus had said and make sense out of it all. "We can see."

CHAPTER SEVENTEEN

MORDRED WOKE FROM A TIRED, uncertain sleep and lay shuddering in the blackness. He had slept once after the woman left him, heavily and without dreams, and after that he had known no time, morning or night, only brief dozes and dreadful awakenings. The cold of the stones seeped up into him, as cold as the rending pain in his heart.

He dreaded the end. No, rather he dreaded how long the end would take. How many hours, how many days would he endure before he breathed his last breath and lay to become a pile of moldering bones in this little storeroom? He was dizzy when he tried to rise, and flashes of pain seared all through his head, no longer only where the sword had hit him. Hunger had attacked him earlier with raging strength, but now he felt only a low, weak emptiness deep in his stomach. He was tired, so tired.

Why? was all his exhausted mind could cry. *Why—why . . .*

He heard the swishing shuffle of footsteps in the hall and tensed unconsciously. It was the first he had heard from the woman since she left him. Was she coming back?

But they never halted, only fading into whispers and then silence. Twice more he heard them pass by before he slept.

Hours later he woke again, a half-waking, dark and sluggish. He was aware in a listless way of the footsteps drawing near. A small clicking noise sounded through his dull haze as he slipped back into dreams.

~

Fiona stumbled in the heavy snow.

"Careful," panted Marcus anxiously.

It was awkward going for both, with her arm supporting him around the waist and his wrapped around her shoulder. She would have gone alone, but she knew he would never let her do that. And besides, she doubted she could find the house on her own.

"How far is it?" she asked him.

Marcus shrugged, the movement bumping him hard against her. "Maybe two miles, maybe three. I never actually saw it myself, but—but I do know roughly where it is," he added hastily as Fiona's mouth opened.

She did not argue. If they were lost later, there would be time enough for that. "Marcus, please let us go back to the road. I know you wanted to cut straight up the mountain, but in this snow, it is not saving us time at all."

Marcus laughed reluctantly. "Of course."

They retraced their steps back to the point where they had left the path for the woods and knee-deep drifts of snow. The sky had clouded over, a silky-grey day with slow star-flakes rocking on the air. The wind was soft and penetrating out in the open, and Fiona felt its cold and longed to hurry; but Marcus' hobbling pace could not be quickened.

The path, heading straight for a while, bent south-east again. "Please, Fiona." Marcus halted and gestured to the woods on their right. "Let's go through this time, just this time. The snow doesn't look as deep, and the path makes such a long loop around here, it will save us a quarter of an hour . . . "

He was ready to go on pleading, but she touched his hand.

"Yes, Marcus," she said, and they turned into the trees.

He had been right; the snow was less deep in this area, whether because the trees were thicker, or the fall had simply been lighter. They made a quick traversal of it and were coming out onto the path beyond when they heard the call coming near at hand over the light wind. "Mordred . . . Mordred!"

There was a deadness to the call—a flatness. They gained the slick, trodden surface of the path and saw Therelane Grey tramping out of the trees opposite, some ways further up. He saw them at the same moment and started in surprise.

"Marcus," he said. "What are you doing?"

"Why aren't you with your group?" Marcus retorted.

"How do you know I am not?" Therelane demanded.

"Because you're the first person we've heard calling at all, and we should have been hearing three or four."

"I told them I was coming back to cover this area again." Therelane's shoulders drooped. "I thought I might—might try looking in the Wilds a little."

"The Wilds!" exclaimed Marcus. "Therelane, not by yourself you wouldn't! Besides, why on earth would he—"

"That's what they said to me," snapped Therelane bitterly. "But Mordred wasn't acting right. He wasn't acting like himself. Who knows what he would have done? Maybe his reason left him. Maybe he did go wandering in the Wilds, forgetting his brother's own accident, forgetting everything he'd ever heard!"

"Listen, Therelane." Marcus stepped forward earnestly, forgetting to lean on Fiona. His leg gave way and he staggered back towards her. "We're looking for Mordred, too," he continued when he had caught his breath. "And we have a good idea of where he might be. Come with us, Therelane."

Therelane looked at them dubiously. "Where?"

"The black house," said Marcus. "The one east of the castle. It's too long to explain, Therelane. I'll tell you as we go."

Therelane hesitated.

Marcus forged purposefully down the path, dragging Fiona behind. Slowly, Therelane fell into step beside them.

~

They broke out of the pine boughs that swept low over the little crooking path and stood looking at the black house. It was almost evening, and the sky was darkening overhead; toward the west the greyness blushed faintly, a whisper of the sinking sun.

"It is so large!" Marcus said, staring at the house curiously. "See how it folds over the land, like a spider, or a sleeping worm, as if it speaks of swallowing the mountain."

Fiona felt a coldness touch her as he spoke—maybe at the wind, maybe at the truth of his words. The dark walls rising up against the snow carried a whisper of menace, and try as she might she could not will the uneasiness away.

"We shall get nowhere by looking at it," said Therelane finally, and it was as though he had snapped some spell that the sight of the house had cast over all of them. They moved quickly up to the large, carven door.

Fiona reached out at once to take the handle yet drew back her hand suddenly with a quick shiver. It was but a half-formed thought, one that comes suddenly and without call, that the door could not possibly open; and with it came the vague, unsettled feeling that it would not be wise to even try.

Therelane walked boldly past her and turned the handle with a hard shove, and the door flung itself open with a startling, wild swiftness. "Come," he said, and led the way in.

The stillness slid over them with the shutting of the door. They wandered slowly through the rooms, hesitant and overwhelmed with the vastness of the house. Room after room: most of them empty, or nearly so. Some had neatly ordered furniture and tapestry-hung walls, though they were all covered in dust.

"What a deserted place," said Marcus aloud, breaking the uncomfortable silence.

No one answered. The silence returned eerier than before.

"Maybe," Therelane suggested after a while, "we should go separately for a little? We could cover more ground quicker."

"No," said Fiona quickly, "please, no. I do not want to split up—not in this place. 'Tis far too easy to get lost."

"All right," Therelane assented unwillingly. "I suppose . . . "

"Look!" cried Marcus, breaking in. He pointed at the ground. "Someone has been here recently. See the boot prints!"

And there, in the dust that was edging the hallway, were several clearly defined prints of a booted foot.

"It must be Mordred," said Marcus firmly, and they pressed on, more hopefully than before.

Their searching took them further and further down, and they found themselves in the region of the cellar.

"Look," said Fiona softly, in surprise. "There are torches burning down here."

Marcus limped over to one door, the upper half marred with a square iron grating. He attempted to peer in—"Too dark"—and turned the handle. It gave a cold click of stone on stone and swung outward. "Smells like apples," he added appreciatively with a long sniff, as he leaned on the door and looked around.

The room was quite small and bare to the very corners. Whatever apples had once filled it were no longer there. "I'm hungry," Marcus murmured, taking another long inhalation of the lingering aroma. He bent down for a minute, rubbing at a dark spot on the stone ground.

"Marcus," said Therelane.

"Sorry," said Marcus, attempting to straighten. "Fiona—would you—" He reached out gratefully for her arm and pulled himself up to his feet.

"That's an odd stain there on the floor." He nodded to the place where he had been scratching. "Brownish, looks almost as though it might have been blood."

Therelane shrugged and pushed the door to again. They moved away down the hall.

~

He had woken again, desperate, frantic to get out. He stumbled dizzily to his feet, hurled himself against the door, and it gave. He fell headlong into the hall.

He lay there for one instant, bewildered, and then wrenched himself to his knees and looked behind him at the door. It was open. He blinked away dark spots, rubbed his hand across his eyes, and it was still open. There, beyond it, was the room he had lain in moments before.

How? For had he not tried the door, so many times?

And then he remembered the little click just as he had fallen asleep: a noise like the sound of a latch releasing.

The questions swarmed dimly in his mind, battering one another like a host of blind moths. She must have opened the door, the woman of the rough hair and dark, angry eyes. Except that she would never have opened the door for him. Fenris would have opened it for him, but Fenris was not here. His gaze drifted puzzled across the empty room. If she had come to mock him, to torment him, or to make a final end of him, he could understand; instead, she had left him a way of escape . . .

It did not matter, he thought, struggling to push through the confusion in his dulled mind. It did not matter how or why. He must get out.

He stumbled up to his feet in a quick, scrambling movement, the effort surprisingly easier than he expected. Almost before he knew it, he was walking, his legs weak but steady enough beneath him. Where they were taking him, he did not know; only when he reached the foot of a stairwell did he realize that he had been following the sound of the woman's departure from his prison-room.

Of course, she would have gone back upstairs. Away from the cellars.

Mordred hesitated before the narrow, curving flight, uncertain whether he could manage it, and flung himself forward before the hesitation could turn to fear. They were steep and bewildering, and after his first wild exertion they seemed to never end. His legs quaked under him, his breath whistled with strain; with each step he thought he could go no further, but he was past the point of stopping.

Step after step. The cold stones of the stairwell brushed beneath his hand, the only real thing remaining through his daze of will. And then, without warning, it was no longer stone, but wood, and he raised his foot, but there was no step before it. He had reached the top. His knees buckled, but he could not fall, must not fall, terrified that if he fell again, he would not get back up.

And he did not fall.

He walked down a passage he did not recognize, turned into a second, and was staring at the archway of the room of scrolls. Lightheaded with excitement, he shut his eyes, willing back the memories of his wanderings through the house.

They came in fits and starts; he followed them slowly, knowing he must not rush. Whenever he could not remember which way to go, he waited, waited for the memory to return and certainty to come, and walked on. At last, he came to the hall with one window and the door at the far end.

The world listed and whirled around him, turning white at the edges, a storm of heady joy and fear that he would be caught when he was so, so close. He reeled, gripped the wall, and clung to it until the whirling receded. Then he lunged for the door.

He slammed against it, too dizzy to halt himself. A moment of fumbling with the knob, a convulsive tug—and he was standing out in the deep snow, the icy wind rushing into his nostrils and the first stars coming out into the twilit sky.

He reached down, slowly, slowly, the world tilting and converging on his ears, and brought up a handful of the cold flakes. For a moment he stared at them, forgetting what he had meant to do with them. They were so light and delicate, like dandelion thistles in his palm; it must have been a recent fall. And then the thistles sank in on themselves, dissolving, turning to water.

Water.

He put the snow to his dry lips. The frozen trickle down his throat, and the cold night all around him, seemed to shake all his deadened senses into aliveness. He took a second mouthful, and a third, and with a quick, roused shiver staggered forward to the beckoning trees.

They closed about him in a muddle of moonlit patterns. His feet carried him on and on, where, he did not know. Sometimes he lurched and all but fell, sometimes stood in a daze for minutes at a stretch before the inner urgency surged up and impelled him forward.

At last his legs gave out under him, and he found himself face down in the snow. He shuddered away from the cold, but the movement sent him deeper into a pit of blackness, and he did not come out of it again.

CHAPTER EIGHTEEN

THERELANE WALKED SWIFTLY THROUGH THE dark night of the mountain. He wanted desperately to intercept the men before they reached the Kenhelms' house, but he knew it was far too late by now. The sun had set hours ago while they roamed the old black house.

"Laufeia," he called, flinging the door open.

She turned, a slight, pale figure, the firelight glimmering red over her long braid. "Who are you?"

Of course, she wouldn't recognize him. He had seen her only that once, when they came to her door yesterday. "I am Therelane Grey."

"Oh." She spoke wearily, as though nothing mattered.

He glanced behind her and saw that Fenris was standing by the fire, very still, his back half-turned, his hands covering his face.

"They came?"

"Aye," she said.

"And they did not find him."

That was not even a question. She gave no answer.

"Laufeia," he began hoarsely, and found his voice failing as their grief touched him and he felt his own fruitless efforts more keenly. "I—I feel your pain as my own," he said at last. "Mordred was my friend—my only friend. I do not know how I shall bear living without him. But I promise you, Laufeia, I will do this for you. I am not bound to the castle labor. I have no work of any kind, since my family is rich and asks none. Therefore, this shall be my work: I will continue to seek

Mordred, although the others must cease. I shall not stop until I have found him, even if it be his body and no more. Whether it takes me a day or a year or ten years, I will find him." Again his voice choked away in his throat.

There were no tears on Laufeia's cheeks, but they were bright and full in her eyes as she said, "I am glad to know that Mordred had a friend. Thank you, Therelane."

~

"Kenneth," said Marianne in relief as he entered. "You were gone so long. You didn't—?"

Kenneth shook his head. "Didn't find him." He shrugged off his coat and walked to warm his hands at the fire.

"I'm sorry, Kenneth," she said softly, and came up behind him to put a hand against his back.

"I feel so—"

"What?" she asked when he did not go on.

He tried to sort his thoughts out. He did not want to tell her, but it had been eating away at him for long enough. "I feel so bad, Marianne. I never liked him. I could even say I disliked him, and without much of a reason at that. Even after he started acting warmer towards us, I never attempted to mend the prejudice I'd built up against him. I . . . I just let it sit there. I didn't speak rudely to him the way the foreman did, but I never gave him a kind word either. And then, so suddenly, he was gone, without a chance for me to make things right. And when I saw Fenris' face this evening when we ended the search, I thought if it had been Jerithan—" He halted quickly.

She was quiet, but he felt her nod. He glanced down at her, at her pale, pointed face and her red hair rich and glistening under the cast of the fire, drawn back smooth into a knot behind her head; at her slender fingers twitching by her side; and he felt a deep rush of gladness for her, for her life. Life that suddenly seemed as fragile and golden as the first spring buttercups. He bent down and kissed her. "I am glad you are with me, Marianne," he whispered. "And that you are alive."

~

Jerithan watched them. He had a sudden, shifting, deep feeling that something was wrong. They had not really talked to him about the search for Mordred Kenhelm, but he felt it now, the wrongness, the tilting in the world. "Is Mordred dead?"

He knew they could not know whether Mordred were dead or not, unless they had found him.

Kenneth turned sharply. "Jerithan? I didn't notice you." He hesitated, dropping his arms from around Marianne, and came to sit down next to Jerithan. "We don't know whether he is or not."

"Then why do you talk like he is?"

"We—we're not looking for him any longer, that's why."

"Why not?" demanded Jerithan, angry at their stupidity.

"Jerithan, we don't know. But the chances that he could have survived three nights out in the snow, especially if he were trapped and injured somewhere, are so small. We've scoured the mountain, and there's a limit to how long they will let us leave the castle work. There's no point in looking further."

Jerithan remembered Mordred Kenhelm's laughing, mobile face, smiling in eyes and mouth as he teased Jerithan and Sandy. "I liked Mordred," he said, a sense of hurt and rebellion swelling in him—against Kenneth partly, against that thing called death.

"I'm sorry, Jerithan." Kenneth put a gentle arm around him.

"You didn't." Jerithan knew his voice was accusing, and he didn't care. "You didn't like him at all."

"I know, Jerithan." Kenneth was tense against Jerithan, his eyes dark and withdrawn, and Jerithan sensed emotions roiling in him that he could only dimly grasp and barely name. Guilt, regret, others. "I wish I had. And it's too late now."

Jerithan's anger washed away. He burrowed deeper into Kenneth's arms. "It doesn't matter," he whispered, hoping to comfort his brother in any possible way. "I still love you."

Kenneth's shoulders shook, and a damp cheek touched Jerithan's.

He hadn't meant to make him cry.

~

Jerithan stared out the window. It was a strange sort of day; the sun could not seem to make up its mind whether it would shine or not. It teetered back and forth between bursts of light and grey cloud. Jerithan wished it would stay gloomy, the way he felt.

"Marianne," he said, "can I go on a walk?"

He was allowed to walk around alone now, as long as he told them where he was going and when he would come back.

"Yes," said Marianne absently.

She forgot to ask him where he was going, and he was glad. Because, for the first time, he did not know where. He simply wanted to walk, and walk, until he could not think anymore.

He turned north when he reached the fork in the path. A few scattered snowflakes tumbled down around him occasionally, though whether they were falling from the sky or wafting down from the trees could not have been said. Jerithan stuck his tongue out, trying to catch one on it, but they were much too few and far between.

He cupped a mound of snow in his mittened hands, rolled it into a ball, and threw it aimlessly at a nearby tree. He continued doing it as he walked, enjoying the sense of accomplishment when he hit his marks. As he formed yet another and squinted at its designated target, something dark just beyond the tree caught his eye, and he trudged towards it, thinking it might be an injured animal; it did not look like a stick, but neither was it moving.

It was not an animal.

Jerithan stared at Mordred. The young man was lying with his face half-buried in the snow. He was white as death, his dark hair hanging in stark relief over his forehead, and Jerithan was sure he must be dead.

But even as he stared in captivated horror, Mordred's shoulders jerked spasmodically, and he fell back limp.

Jerithan was running, running over to him, grabbing him by the arm and shaking him. "Mordred! Mordred!"

Mordred stirred, and his slack body stiffened a little. His eyes flickered open and stared at Jerithan, clear grey like the snow-flecked sky. "What . . . you doing here?" he murmured.

"I was throwing snowballs," said Jerithan. "What happened to you? Why didn't they find you?"

Mordred closed his eyes and sank back. "I was in the house."

"Get up, Mordred!"

"Too . . . tired."

"You don't want to stay here, do you?"

"No." Mordred opened his eyes and smiled a little. "But if you could find your older brother or someone, it would help me considerably."

Jerithan frowned. "I don't want to leave you here."

"I'll be fine." Mordred gave that gentle, reassuring smile. "You're a fine strong boy. You can hurry."

"Try to move around," Jerithan ordered, turning to leave. "You need to get warm if you can."

He thought he heard Mordred laughing faintly as he rushed back to the road and fled up it towards the castle. He must get Kenneth, fast . . .

A flicker of movement whipped past his eye, something tall and eerie in the shadow of the trees. He cast a glance back over his shoulder, thinking of scavenging animals that might find Mordred, but saw nothing. Again he broke into a run.

~

Therelane strode doggedly down the path, his narrow brows met in a grim line above his eyes. Oblivious to all but the road at his feet, he barely heard the sound of flying feet until he and the boy ran straight into one another.

"Jerithan Denholm?" Therelane uttered in bewilderment, staring at the wild-eyed boy.

"I—found—Mordred," panted Jerithan, his small, stocky chest heaving. "I'm going to get Kenneth."

Therelane blinked and stared at him again. "What?"

"I found Mordred!" Jerithan shouted.

"Impossible!"

"You don't believe me?" Jerithan turned to march down the road again.

"No, Jerithan! Wait! He is—alive?"

"Yes," said Jerithan, turning.

"Where?"

"Down that way, a little way before the fork. He's lying in the trees off the road."

"Go on, get your brother," said Therelane. "And anyone else who will come." He whirled about, even as Jerithan took off again towards the castle.

~

It is time. You must kill him. Now.

She had stood watching long enough.

You weaken your resolve rather than strengthening it. The boy has gone, and soon the rest will come. If they find him alive, the truth will at once be out. You will have to go back; you will fail; and what then?

The first time she had felt the pangs of unease strike her was when he had spoken at her doorstep. She had thought he was the messenger, and that had been her first mistake . . .

Then he had waited for her coming, so proud and young, and she had seen his vulnerability that shone out all the stronger because he would have hidden it from her; and she found she could not slay him. She had enjoyed mocking him, yes, even inflicting pain upon him, but the final stroke—she could not bear to deliver the stroke. So she had wounded him instead and watched him as he slept, fooling herself that she cared not what became of him.

She had said to herself that she could let him die alone.

All the while her heart betrayed her, for she could not let him alone.

You weaken. Would you go back to the ways of the Vanvar Legeata, having rejected them? Would you own yourself under his hand again?

He had been lying in a different place when she went to look at him again, hard by the wall where the light could not reach him, so she had opened the door, satisfied herself that he was still alive—and left. And she was not quite sure how the door had failed to wholly shut behind her.

As she had mounted the stairs, she had realized her slip and checked an instant. Then she reasoned that there was no basis for him to try it again; he was too weak and had surely tried it so many times already. And she told herself, for the second time, that she would not go to look at him again.

But foreboding had stirred in her that evening, compelling her to go back, and when she went, the empty room did not surprise her. She had known all along, in her heart, he would be gone.

She set her lips and strode out of the thicket towards the dark figure on the ground. It was time.

CHAPTER NINETEEN

THERELANE RAN. HE HAD NEVER run so hard or so long. Snow shot up around his feet and the wind ripped into his chest, and as he plunged headlong into the woods a branch swished straight across his face. He pulled to a halt, feeling the tears smarting into his eyes.

Angrily he broke the branch and hurled it away from him, and hurried on through the woods, scanning for a man's form. He was drawing near the fork; he must be there soon. For a second or two his heart rose in his throat with the fear that he would not be there after all. But then he circled around toward the road, and movement caught his eye. He turned and came over a little white rise and saw Mordred on the ground. And over him stood a woman.

Tall for a woman she was, six feet or more, and her body was lean and strong like a wildcat. Like a tigress over her kill, indeed, she stood over Mordred, her tawny hair falling rough over her shoulders, her eyes dark and menacing.

"Stand back from him!" he cried fiercely. He pointed an accusing finger at her.

She threw her head back in defiance. "And why must I do that, son of *ugthoda*?"

"I know not what harm you mean him, but I tell you, stand back!"

She gave a fierce, high laugh. "Who says that I mean him harm? See you any weapon in my hand?"

Therelane took a second look at her, and indeed, she held no weapon; but the conviction did not leave him. He had seen her head come up and her eyes lock on his like a predator who warns against interference with his prey. "I think you do mean him harm, weapon or no. And how am I to know what you may have hidden in your skirt?"

She cast him an odd, sideways look, and a bitter smile lifted one side of her mouth. "So, you are neither coward nor gull. How came you here so swiftly?—for I would know before I slay you. I expected that the boy could fetch no one before an hour had gone."

"If you speak of Jerithan Denholm, he came upon me on the road. I was not at the castle."

"Of course. 'Tis my own ruin for forgetting that. Well, I have bided long enough. Now you both must die, and so much the worse for that; but I dare not delay."

"What do you mean? Why must you kill either of us?"

"Why?" she repeated with a scornful look. Then it faded and she seemed to drowse in thought a moment. "I was given a task, *rigonharis*," she said at last. "What it is, and from whom, it matters not. But its nature demands secrecy, and secrecy I have been denied. First by him, whom I have sought to slay these three times, and even now my resolve eludes me. And secondly by you, whom I know, son of Guron Grey. Your family is plagued by a curse."

"So?" said Therelane. Why she would speak of the curse at this of all times, he knew not.

"Na, 'tis nothing. Perhaps someday you shall learn the nature of that curse, that is all. But if I am to keep my oath, you both shall die; for he knows too much, and it will be my certain end, and you knew me for a danger when you first saw me. If all the village learns my existence, I must flee."

"You—would not," he stammered.

"Would I not? I am a fair hand with a blade, son of Guron—" and suddenly it was out, the knife, glittering in her hand like a pretty thing. "I might land it in your chest now." And she lifted it, measuring the distance with her eyes.

"They will . . . " He struggled to speak. His head was light, as though stuffed with wool, knowing that he was on the edge of death. "They will see my body; they will know I was slain by the hand of man and not beast. They will seek you out and find you."

"They will not." She spoke with a cold, immutable certitude. "I will take you to my house and lock your bodies therein, and they will not be found before your bones have crumbled into dust."

"Your house?" And it burst upon him with a quietly blinding clarity. "The black house."

"The black house," she repeated, mockery lilting her tone. "None of you in your foolishness dreamed that there might be one living there, did you? None of you thought to search it out."

"One did." Therelane flung the words at her, his desperation half a hope to stall her and that knife in her hand, half a wish to merely call her wrong. To show her that she was not as great as she thought.

She was rolling the hilt of the blade between her fingers. Her hands halted suddenly. "What are you saying?"

"Marcus thought to search it. He and I and Fiona went yesterday. We looked through every room of that house."

She appeared surprised, and even laughed. "So. A fine mis-crossing of paths that was! I was gone out that afternoon and evening, and he must have escaped before you found him. Ai, but it matters not. If you think those tidings will stop me, think once more, son of Guron. I have places to hide that no man can know." With a toss of her heavy, lion-like mane, she lifted the knife and caressed it with the palm of her hand.

"Do not!" he begged. "Whatever this task may be, it cannot be worth a life!"

A slight sneer passed over her features. "And how if I vowed to kill him—knowing that he would betray all in an instant if I did not—and let you go, binding you with an oath of silence? How would you answer then?"

He was mute, seeking to understand her meaning at first; and then he started and stared at her, stricken.

"Speak! I am giving you a choice: leave him to his death and never tell anyone or die with him now. And hurry, for I will not wait. But it will rest easier with me knowing that I did not kill two men this day."

He recovered his voice, though it shook as he spoke. "Never tell?"

"The price is too high, yes? Nay, I will not wait for an answer from you. I do not trust that eye of yours. You loved him too well to let his death go in silence." She tested the point of the knife on her finger. "I will kill him first, lest I succumb to the temptation again."

Therelane's eyes flew down to Mordred, wondering for the first time if he were even aware. It did not seem so; he lay so motionless, his eyes closed, his breath coming faint and slow. He never shivered or twitched as the shining metal lifted above his body. Perhaps he was unconscious. Or perhaps he was just too near to care.

She stooped, knelt beside him. The knife quivered in her fingers like a live thing. She set it against his shoulder-blades.

Therelane could not move or speak.

The knife rested there for one second—two—three—

She straightened slowly, turning the knife over and over in her hands. "Nay, it is too late now," she said softly.

And her face that she lifted to Therelane's was both sad and proud; and there was something strangely beautiful in that unbeautiful countenance.

"I knew that he was my doom when I first beheld him. It may be that the Vanvar Legeata put him in my way, knowing I could not slay him, for I have run from him too long. And so it comes to pass. I shall go, and he shall live." All this time, as she spoke, she had still been turning the knife over and over in her hands; and suddenly she let it slip through, and it fell with a light sound at her feet.

"Farewell, son of Guron."

She turned and walked away slowly through the trees.

Therelane lowered himself to the ground, shaking. He wanted strangely to weep; yet he did not. He knelt there, his hands clenching in the snow, until he heard voices suddenly close at hand, and Braegon was crying, "Here! Here they are!" and "Steady, Therelane, now what is amiss?"

He felt a quietness washing over him, like the sense of a dream fading. The world cleared and was bright again. "Naught, Braegon. It is all well now. Mordred?"

"They are seeing to him."

Mordred pushed away the hands as they attempted to lift him up. "I can walk," he muttered blearily.

"Nay, you'll not walk," said Mr. Earle.

"Fenris?"

"I am here, Mordred." Fenris was at his side. Mordred reached out blindly and caught his brother's shoulder with one hand.

"What happened?" Braegon demanded as Therelane stood up.

Therelane was silent a little. "It is too much to think on now," he said finally. "I do not want to think about it yet. Let you ask me another time, Braegon."

~

"What was it like, Braegon?" Therelane asked as they made their way under the noon sun to the Kenhelm house. "What was it like when Jerithan came with the news?"

"What was it like?" Braegon laughed. "I myself only know what I felt, and that was as though my heart had become the sun and would burn a hole straight through me. Half of me, that soldierly half, could not believe him at first. There was not a word among any one of us, and the only thing that broke the silence was the foreman's hammer that he dropped. And then we looked around like five sets of fools, blundering with our words and asking what should be done. Thankfully, Fred was clear enough. 'We must go get him,' he said, and so go we did.

"As for Fenris, his face was alit with joy such as I have never seen. I think his heart knew that Mordred was not yet dead. It was good, Therelane, to see him so glad. I would give the wealth of a king to see that look on his face again."

Aside from Braegon's earnest, shining-clear words, all the walk to the Kenhelms and the flurries of activity when they reached it were a blur for Therelane. He stood blankly in a corner, aware that there was to-do and comings and goings, and that at one point he was listening to Mr. Earle's quiet, steady voice asking, "How long were you lying there?" and Mordred's murmuring answer, "An hour, maybe—'twas near dawn when I fell, I think."

Then all the noise and confusion had faded away, and again it seemed like he was coming out of a dream. He heard the fire distantly crackling in the other room, and saw Mordred lying on a straw tick in the corner with one hand over his eyes; Laufeia was tucking blankets in around him.

Therelane hurried over. "Mordred—Mordred?"

"Aye," Mordred murmured in answer. His hand slipped down and his eyes opened to fix on Therelane. "Therelane. What happened?"

"When?"

"Between the time Jerithan found me and when the others arrived."

"The woman came."

"She did, then—I wondered. Did she hurt you?"

"Nay, Mordred."

"What happened? Did they drive her off?"

"No; she—she left, Mordred."

"She left." Mordred was quiet for a time. "Yes; I remember how it was."

Therelane said nothing.

Mordred spoke again. "Therelane?"

"What?"

"I'm sorry I did not tell you."

"Tell me what?"

"When you asked me . . . what was wrong."

"Oh, that. Nay, Mordred, it does not matter. You did nothing wrong."

"No," countered Mordred with a small, wry smile. "I was quite stupid. I ought to have told you then and there, Therelane."

"It turned out all right in the end," Therelane said earnestly, touching Mordred's hand. "How are you? Hurting at all? Any injuries?"

"I am fine, Therelane." Though the shadows under his eyes told otherwise. He fell asleep not five minutes later, his hand loosely clasping Therelane's.

"He is just tired," said Laufeia softly, coming up behind him. "He'll likely sleep till tomorrow noon, but he won't be much the worse after that."

"I'll come tomorrow, then." Therelane stood up, glancing down at Mordred's relaxed form. "If you don't mind," he added quickly.

"Mind?" Laufeia looked almost as though she would laugh. "You are welcome here any time you choose to come, Therelane. Even if I wanted to keep you out, I am sure Mordred would not hear of it!"

Therelane left the house feeling peculiarly happy, as though Laufeia's words had left a soothing touch on an ache that was still there, though fading.

But it was fading. Not often now did he have those pangs of loneliness he used to have. He had almost begun to feel as though he were accepted, welcomed. As though he were one of Ceristen, in the way he had never been. Oh, if only Mordred knew all he had done for him! Therelane longed to speak of it, but he also felt too shy, as if the telling would be to thrust himself in some way on Mordred's kindness.

And perhaps Mordred did know, or at least guessed. The thought left a still greater warmth in Therelane's heart, one that stayed hovering around it all the walk back to his own house.

"You're quite improved these days," Irene observed dryly as he passed her in the hall.

He turned, startled. “Improved?”

Irene sniffed and shrugged. “I wouldn’t say you’re Thireler the Conqueror, but you’re a far cry from the sorry mope you used to be.”

He was unsure what to say. Things like compliments she brushed off. “Does it matter to you so much, Irene?”

She had already half-turned, in her brisk way, but a small smile whisked across her face. “If I’d had the time or inclination to change you, I would have. As it is, I have someone else to thank for it. Goodnight, Therelane.”

CHAPTER TWENTY

FIONA BENT OVER MARCUS. "HOW does it feel?"

"All right." Marcus shifted listlessly.

The door slammed open with a force that made them jump.

"What's going on?" cried Peony from the bedroom.

Bardrick came running in, snow spilling from his shoulders and boots. "They found him," he gasped. "Mordred."

Marcus, who had got up on one elbow, fell back openmouthed. "They—what?" he uttered.

Fiona was on her feet, dizzy with the surprise, the one question she could not form banging against the walls of her mind: *alive?*

"He will be all right, they think." Bardrick leaned against the wall to catch his breath. "Mr. Earle said he seemed to have hit his head, but that was not too severe, and it is on the mend. Other than that, he was not so badly off."

Marcus waited for nothing more, but released a wild, shrill yell and flung his blanket into the air. He lay back with an air of satisfaction and let Fiona and Peony fuss over him. "That felt good," he declared. "Now I can die happy."

"Nonsense," said Peony. "I don't want to hear you or anyone talking about dying for the next few years."

Marcus summoned an apologetic cough. "Understandable, sister."

Fiona withdrew to the corner. She must have a little solitude in order to command the gladness that had risen so piercingly in her. She stood alone there for a little, letting it settle upon her with its bright ache, and she wept a little, too, silent tears of joy, and of release. When they ebbed away, the happiness swelled up high and then higher, and she knew that she must have an outlet for it.

"I am going to Laufeia." She snatched up her shawl and ran lightly out the door.

~

A hot morning's sun prickled the back of Therelane's neck. He hesitated and rapped twice on the wood.

"Aye?" The tall young man who opened the door cocked an eyebrow at him. "Do I know you?"

"You're doing better," Therelane said gladly.

Mordred gave a sharp shrug. "I ought to have gone to work today, but Fenris left without me."

"You slept till half-noon!" called Laufeia from within.

"That's an improvement on yesterday," said Therelane, "when I believe you didn't wake till dusk."

Mordred's smile flashed out. "I don't remember a minute of it."

"You were asleep," Laufeia returned, appearing behind him. "What do you expect?"

"Did she really succeed in keeping you home?" Therelane asked, transferring his attention to Mordred's earlier remark.

"Not without difficulty," said Mordred a little smugly.

"I argued with him for nigh an hour," said Laufeia with an exasperated sigh and turned back into the kitchen again.

"You ought to listen to her, you know." Therelane felt it somehow his duty to take Mordred to task on this. "You really aren't well enough to work all day at the castle yet."

Mordred's lips thinned. "You are not in my body," he retorted, "and can hardly know how I feel." He tossed his head as though to dismiss the subject. "What did you come for?"

"Oh—I do not know. Well, if restriction is so irking you, why do we not walk around awhile? Not too far or too long; just to get out of the house."

Mordred glanced defiantly at Laufeia, waiting for an objection.

"I do not mind," said Laufeia, "so long as you come back for dinner. Make sure he does not tire himself, Therelane."

"I will not," said Mordred as he walked out the door.

"Where are we going?" asked Therelane in a short time. Mordred had set a swift pace and seemed to be heading in a very purposeful direction.

Mordred glanced briefly at him. "The black house."

~

"Why did you want to come here?" Therelane looked around at the musty hall they had entered.

"I do not know." Mordred frowned a little, brushing his fingers against the edge of the wall. "I thought I might find my knife in that room of scrolls. I dropped it there, when she took me."

"What room of scrolls?" Therelane followed Mordred, thrusting aside the cobwebs that reached hungrily at his face.

Mordred halted just under an arched doorway, the door beside it hanging ajar. The parchments lay heaped on the floor, dingy and crumbling, odd little trinkets scattered among them. Therelane edged up beside him to see better.

"Where did these come from?" he asked.

"The castle," Mordred answered, and moved forward, glancing this way and that, delicately pushing the scrolls aside.

Therelane shifted uneasily. The woman's terrible, tigress-cold face swam before his eyes, and he half-expected to hear footsteps approaching down the hall. He wandered a short way and examined a narrow table situated against the wall, a few scrolls strewn loosely across it and one sheet lying flat with the penned words *Mordred Kenhelm* and *house of Ithera*. One of the scrolls was written like a letter, but a hasty, unfinished, and discarded letter; Therelane did not try to decipher its blotted contents. None of the other proximate scrolls were in the same hand.

"Here it is," said Mordred's voice, and Therelane looked to see his friend lifting a long, double-edged knife from the sea of scrolls.

"There it is!" Therelane echoed in relief.

Mordred nodded and let the weapon slide into his belt but showed no indication to depart. Thoughtfully, he bent and picked up something else from the floor, a little oval stone carved with foreign runes, and rubbed it in an absent way between his hands.

Silence sank in. Therelane looked around the room, comprehension settling on him. "She took these things from the castle. Is that why you were coming here?"

"Aye; that is why."

Therelane was quiet, remembering the woman and all the strange fear and emotion of the morning two days ago. Earlier he had not wanted to think of it; he had tried to shut it out. But here, in this dead, silent house, he could not help but remember.

"A terrible woman," he said aloud, his voice falling flat on the still air. "Why did she take them? What was her purpose here?"

"I do not know," said Mordred softly. He held the stone in his fingers with distant gaze. "I think maybe we will never know. But in the end, she let me go. I would not think too hard of her, Therelane."

Therelane said nothing. Mordred's head was up, his grey eyes alight and keen with something that he was looking on that Therelane could not enter into. He tossed the small carving lightly into the air, once, twice, and let it land with a whir of rustling parchment on the ground.

Therelane took his hand. "Come, Mordred. Let us leave this place."

Mordred glanced around the room, in an almost regretful sort of way; and then he turned and followed Therelane obediently out.

So they left the black house behind.

"They'll have to get a party of several in there, to return all those scrolls and whatnot to the castle," said Therelane as they walked back. "Someday."

Mordred murmured assent.

"You could go back with them."

Mordred did not seem to hear at first; then he started and shook his head. "I think I bade farewell to it there," he said. "I will not go back again."

~

Jerithan was going to the Kenhelms.

Marianne hadn't let him go yesterday; she had said Mordred was still getting better and Jerithan would only bother him. Jerithan didn't believe he would bother him, but he had stayed anyway. Today, Marianne still had not wanted him to go, but Kenneth had said, "Let him, Marianne. He found him, after all. He deserves to see Mordred if anyone does."

But he did not have to reach the house, after all, to find him.

"Mordred!" Jerithan shouted, as the young man's tall figure approached the crossroads with Therelane close by.

Mordred's head swung up and his face lighted in a wide smile. "Jerithan!" He held his arms out and caught Jerithan up in them, throwing him up as though he had been a ball. Jerithan, who ordinarily hated people besides Kenneth hugging him, did not mind.

"I thought," he said breathlessly as Mordred set him down, "that you were sick."

Mordred scowled lightly and tossed it off with a laugh. "That is what Laufeia thinks. But you see otherwise."

"If you toss a hefty six-year-old boy in the air again," warned Therelane, "I will tell her."

"I do not fear Laufeia," said Mordred with a lofty look. He was panting, however.

"You're getting tired," Therelane insisted. "Don't be throwing him again."

"I am not made of glass," Mordred grumbled.

Jerithan scuffed his feet. He was being ignored.

Mordred glanced down at him. "Come, Jerithan, walk with us," he said. "Unless you are going somewhere else?"

"No," said Jerithan. "I was coming to see you." He fell into step happily beside them, although Mordred's strides were so long that it was impossible for him to keep up without running. But Mordred noticed almost at once and shortened his steps. Jerithan trotted along, feeling Mordred's hand resting on his shoulder, and warm all through.

~

They sat together at supper: the three Kenhelms. Laufeia was conscious of it in a strange way. She looked from Mordred, his hard-set jaw and his grey eyes looking alert and oddly distant in the dim firelight, the little, contented smile perking up one side of his mouth on occasion—to Fenris, his thin, gentle face, the dark forelock of hair and the sensitive mouth that were like Mordred's, his soft, expressive eyes that were ever resting on his brother.

"My face is interesting?" Mordred asked, laughter dancing in his tone.

She answered with a wry smile. "Yes, Mordred; tonight it is."

"And what is so special about tonight, then?"

"Naught, maybe. But you are here, and there is something special about that, even though it is ordinary."

Mordred pushed his chair back a little and leaned on it, his eyes flickering. "I think—because it is ordinary," he said softly. And he got up, as though to leave, and he crossed over to Laufeia, and kissed her gently on the top of the head. Then he turned and walked out of the room.

CHAPTER TWENTY-ONE

THE WIND WAS IN THE trees as Fiona walked up the road and halted on the brow of the hill to watch the sun rise. The morning was clean and luminous, the sun a throbbing ball of white-gold, the fuzzy rays streaming past her into the trees behind.

"Fiona, my lady." The voice spoke behind her.

"Fred!" she said quickly, turning. "A pleasant chance meeting, this."

"It is not a chance meeting, my lady. I hoped to find you."

"I . . . I see." Her voice was a breath in her own ears. Her heart quivered. Why did he seek her out? She did not know—she was afraid she knew—she was still unsure of her own mind.

He took a breath as though to speak.

"Is it—is it not wonderful," she stammered, "that Mordred has been found?" Oh, she was making a fool of herself. *Fiona Segelas, you are no better than a lovesick girl . . .*

His glad, sincere smile came to his face. "It is that. Come, Fiona, I must away to the castle, but will you not walk with me?"

"I will," she answered over the painful threshing of her heart.

They walked in silence, but neither the silence nor the peaceful wind and sunrise were able to calm Fiona's trembling, disordered thoughts.

Did she love him? How was she to know, who knew so little of that kind of love? And could she say him nay if she did not love him; could she hurt him so? She knew that she could not. Yet he would never willingly take to him as a bride one who had no love for him; of that she was sure as well.

Think—you must think. How do you feel towards him? What are your thoughts of him?

He is a good man, a gentle man. He is strong and loving. He is intelligent, yet he is humble, and he longs to learn.

She forced herself to acknowledge the other truths about him, the ones which she would rather have left beneath the surface. *He is indecisive. He cannot speak readily of his own hurts. He—*

"When I see the sun rise, I feel that I might touch the sky, or take flight like a bird to the stars."

"It is a wondrous feeling," Fiona assented. "'Tis why I came out to see it this morn."

He ceased walking suddenly and turned to face her. "I could not speak to you before, not with the sorrow hanging over us all. Fiona Segelas, I love you."

Her heart was no longer trembling and bewildered; it had sailed into a dream where the light was gold and the sea was gold and all that mattered was the strange and wonderful words that had fallen from the lips of the man who stood before her. "You—love me," she repeated, her voice a whisper.

"I love you, Fiona Segelas. I have loved you this past se'ennight and more."

"And—and what sort of an answer do you expect?" she questioned.

His face sobered. "A truthful one, my lady. I have given you my heart, now all I ask is that you tell me yours. I could not let it go unspoken any longer—I must bare it to you."

She was silent. He did not press her to speak.

What is your heart? It is time to learn.

She considered all her acquaintance with Fred, her thoughts flitting from one clear-cut memory to the next with blinding speed. How he had sought her out. How he had spoken with her just outside the door of her house. All she had learned of him that night that they supped with the Thorne family. His comforting of her when she had been distressed. The love in his eyes when he looked at her at the castle—as he looked at her right now.

And then she thought of living each day with this man, and caring for him, and knowing him, and rearing children in their arms, and she knew her answer.

"It is in my heart that I—that I love you, Frederick Thorne." A soft flush of emotion came to her cheeks as she spoke, and she lifted her eyes to his.

He caught his breath as though struck or pained, yet his eyes shone. "Say it again, my lady."

"I love you," Fiona said again, and she knew, with a steady, piercing knowledge, that it was true. She was bound to this man until the end of her days.

She reached out to him, and he took her hands, as though he would have kissed them; but in sudden abandon he gathered her close and set his lips to her brow. "My love," he whispered as the sun shone against them, "will you wed me when the snow has left, and the trees of spring are budding?"

She could scarcely find it in her to speak, so loud was her heart singing. "I will wed you," she said.

They stood so together for a long time, silent, for their joy was too full for the deepest sea of words. The sun shone brightly, and in its heat one droplet formed and rolled down off a branch.

Fiona stirred against him. "Look," she said. "The spring is coming."

Fred laughed. "It will not be for a little while yet, my love," he returned gently. "But it will come."

THE END

To be continued in

THE CLAW

GLOSSARY

Erahar: A stark, mountainous country on the west coast. Survival takes precedence over education for most inhabitants, but the nobility have a rigorous system of literacy and customs.

Rehirne: A small country which abuts Orden's southwest border. With few natural resources, the poverty and mortality rate is high, especially among the impounded orphans.

eghuire: Eraharian word meaning 'sister'.

ugthoda: A type of evil creature that roamed Orden before the days of Thireler the Conqueror.

rigonharis: A term of Rodronian origin meaning "little brave man."

Vanvar Legeata: A term of Rodronian origin meaning "Ruler of the Worlds."

For more information about
Verity A. Buchanan
&
The Village
please visit:

www.verityabuchanan.com
www.facebook.com/VBuchananWrites

For more information about
AMBASSADOR INTERNATIONAL
please visit:

www.ambassador-international.com
@AmbassadorIntl
www.facebook.com/AmbassadorIntl

If you enjoyed this book, please consider leaving us a review on Amazon, Goodreads, or our website.

www.ingramcontent.com/pod-product-compliance
Lightning Source LLC
LaVergne TN
LVHW050626100826
845148LV00011B/1755

* 9 7 8 1 6 4 9 6 0 0 2 3 3 *